Finally, th

Eleanor put ... n
circumstances ... e
sure not to miss a word. For Aunt Daphne's sake, she had to
know about Mr. Jarvis. She felt her body tense.

"Since the party, it has come to my attention that Flint's
source of wealth is not known. He says he is gainfully employed
in shipping, yet he shows no evidence that such an enterprise
supports his ability to gallivant about town every day."

"So he doesn't spend his time with his nose buried in legal
briefs all day like you do." Eleanor could visualize Mrs. Alden
shrugging. "Does that make him a villain?"

"I hope not."

"You may have influence in the courts, but I would think
long and hard about accusing someone of wrongdoing if I
were you." Eleanor imagined Mrs. Alden shaking her finger
at Raleigh as she dispensed such advice.

"Indeed. And I assure you, I express my concerns to you
in the strictest confidence." He exhaled. "I tell you once and
for all, your best laid plans have failed. I am not interested in
Vera, simply because she melts into the wall; nor am I interested in Eleanor, because though she is a fine seamstress, that
is still her station—that of a tradeswoman."

Eleanor flinched.

Tamela Hancock Murray is the award-winning, best-selling author of eight titles for Heartsong Presents, many novellas, and seven Bible trivia books. She shares her home in Virginia with her godly husband and their two beautiful daughters. They stay busy with church, school, cheerleading, scouting, and work. Tamela hopes that her stories of God-centered romance edify and entertain her sisters in Christ. Contact Tamela by e-mailing her at TamelaHancockMurray@juno.com.

Books by Tamela Hancock Murray

HEARTSONG PRESENTS

HP213—Picture of Love
HP408—Destinations
HP453—The Elusive Mr. Perfect
HP501—Thrill of the Hunt
HP544—A Light Among Shadows
HP568—Loveswept
HP598—More Than Friends
HP616—The Lady and the Cad

Love's
Denial

Tamela Hancock Murray

Heartsong Presents

A note from the author:
I love to hear from my readers! You may correspond with me by writing:

Tamela Hancock Murray
Author Relations
PO Box 719
Uhrichsville, OH 44683

ISBN 1-59310-543-6

LOVE'S DENIAL

All scripture quotations are taken from the King James Version of the Bible.

PRINTED IN THE U.S.A.

one

Where is Aunt Daphne? Why isn't she here to meet me? This is the height of rudeness—me traveling all this way to see her—and my aunt off to who knows where.

Eleanor Kerr stood by the vacant fireplace in her aunt's parlor and waved her white silk fan, painted with depictions of exotic birds, in front of her nose. Stirring a small portion of nearby hot air did little to allay the discomfort of Baltimore in the summer. Having just arrived at her aunt's house, she was still dressed in her stiff traveling suit, a condition she was eager to amend.

She lifted a tendril of deep auburn hair that had come loose from her chignon and tucked it back into place. Papa had sent her to Maryland so she could escape the tropical climate in Louisiana—the state they called home. Malaria had killed her mother more than a year ago, a fate that he didn't want for his only daughter. Yet the summer heat felt no less intense in the formal parlor of Aunt Daphne's row house than it had back in her home in Louisiana.

In her heart, Eleanor knew that Papa had other reasons for sending her to Baltimore. As Mama's illness had progressed, Papa had let business matters slide while he spent nearly every penny on doctors who, in the end, could do nothing. Mama's death had left him so lethargic that he had lost all interest in life. Eleanor wished she could have stayed with Papa to lend support as he revitalized his business. But he would not permit her to remain with him. Her new life in

5

Baltimore promised to be quite different than that of a pampered only child. Here, she would be expected to become self-sufficient by learning her aunt's trade—that of a seamstress.

Eleanor fingered the collar of the suit that she had sewn herself. A pleasant and productive pastime would now be the way she would earn her keep, though not the life of her dreams. Thankfully, she possessed both the talent and patience for sewing while she waited to see what the Lord really had in mind.

She increased the motion of her fan, which offered some relief. At least Eleanor's initial period of mourning had passed, so she was no longer required to swelter in a black frock. Not that she minded bearing a little heat and observing the restrictions of mourning. Wearing black had been the least she could do to show the world how much she missed her mother. She was finally becoming accustomed to the muted hues she was now permitted to wear. The dull colors served as a badge for Eleanor to honor her mother. Feeling her eyes mist, Eleanor blinked back tears and forced herself to remember that her dear mama was at home with her heavenly Father.

But for now, earthly matters awaited. Eleanor speculated about reuniting with a relative she hadn't seen in years. They had enjoyed a vigorous correspondence, so Eleanor knew she could expect a certain amount of comfort with her aunt.

Although the youngest of Papa's ten siblings, Daphne was well past her prime to marry and had set up a fine house for herself. The parlor strove mightily to replicate Queen Victoria's palace. A gilded mirror that Eleanor recognized as having once been in Grandmama's house hung from ceiling to floor. It was situated between two front windows of equal height that were dressed in white lace curtains. Eleanor knew without being told that her aunt's choice for winter draperies would be heavy velvet, most likely in a deep blue to reflect the colors in the busy botanical wallpaper that covered all four walls. Along the edges of the walls, hardwood floors gleamed. She could smell the pleasant odor of freshly applied bees-wax. The center of the room was protected from the dirt and grime of shoes by a rug light in both hue and weight as was the fashion for southern homes in the summer. No doubt the covering would be replaced by a lush, dark Oriental rug once the temperatures dipped.

With a gloved hand, she leaned over and ran her left fore-finger along the edge of a table carved from mahogany. She lifted it to her face and recognized that not a speck of dirt sullied the white cotton. No surprise there. Each piece of furniture was polished, and she eyed no visible dust. Out of curiosity, she peered into the top of a table and discovered that she could see her reflection almost as well as if she were looking into a mirror. The house clearly reflected the fussi-ness of the dreary spinster seamstress who was the lady of the house. Eleanor's disposition lent itself to tidiness, but she decided that meeting her aunt's expectations for order would be a challenge.

Lord, I pray that my fears will be unfounded and that Aunt Daphne and I will prove to be kindred spirits. Let my presence here not be a burden upon her. Lead me in Thy will, heavenly Father. In the name of Thy Son, I pray. Amen.

A sense of peace enveloped her. The trip had tired Eleanor. Cutting her glance to a sofa slipcovered in white, she contem-plated taking a seat but thought better of it.

"There you are!"

With a twist of her lace-covered neck, Eleanor turned her face toward the door that led to the entry hall. A redhead who could only be Aunt Daphne breezed into the parlor. She wore a large hat with a brim that seemed to be as wide as the span of Eleanor's arms when outstretched. Earlier that day, Eleanor had donned her traveling dress, a linen affair that was the color of rich coffee flavored with half a cup of thick cream. At the time she had felt stylish even though her current stage of mourning demanded that she wear subdued shades. But now, amid such a flourish of color, she felt downright drab.

"Welcome!" Aunt Daphne glided to her, reached out, and pulled Eleanor to her with a gusto that caught Eleanor by surprise and nearly resulted in her loss of balance.

Eleanor touched the brim of her beige hat to straighten it. She surveyed the floor without moving her head much, hoping that none of the artificial white magnolia flowers on the hat's beige ribbon had become detached and fallen off.

"Thank you." Eleanor trusted that her voice and expression seemed sweet.

Aunt Daphne held her at arm's length. Her green eyes looked Eleanor over and seemed to register approval. "Did you have a good trip?"

"Yes. I found my train compartment agreeable and shared most of the trip with two sisters traveling to New York. They were pleasant enough."

"I'm sorry I'm late in returning. I had planned to be here to greet you upon your arrival. Were you waiting long?" Her charming manner made Eleanor see why her papa said that her aunt had been quite the belle in her younger years. Not that she seemed all that old. Born a decade and a half after Papa, Aunt Daphne seemed younger than her thirty-nine years.

"No, only a few minutes."

"I trust that my driver took good care of you."

"Indeed. Henry was most pleasant."

Aunt Daphne released her grip so she could gesture with her hands. "Mrs. Alden took longer than I expected to choose her lace, and then I had to settle the bill with her son. Honestly, Raleigh Alden is such a vexation. I pity the woman who falls for his handsome face because she will have quite a wretched life with such a miser!"

"If Mr. Alden didn't want to pay the bill, then you can

simply say that you won't provide your services for his mother anymore," Eleanor suggested.

"What? And lose my best patron? Never!"

Eleanor wasn't sure how Mrs. Alden could be Aunt Daphne's best patron if her son didn't want to pay the bill.

"He thought the lace his mother chose was too expensive," Aunt Daphne said in response to her unspoken question. "I had to convince him otherwise. You'd think he couldn't rub two nickels together, when in reality, his is one of the wealthier families in the Baltimore area."

"You certainly have had a difficult afternoon." Eleanor wondered if the events were typical for her aunt.

"Lest you think you've moved into bedlam, let me assure you that every afternoon is not like this one!" When Aunt Daphne removed her hat, Eleanor noticed that it was most astonishing. The hat was burdened with quite a chore in holding up artificial lemons, limes, oranges, and bananas tied together with a bright yellow bow. Eleanor knew she could never carry off such a concoction, but Daphne wore it well.

Her aunt placed the bright yellow creation on the mahogany stand. "Have you eaten?" Without the hat for a distraction, Eleanor noticed that her aunt's face still held the beauty of her youth.

"Yes," Eleanor answered. "I took a meal on the train, thank you."

"Good. Cook gets awfully grumpy when I ask her to prepare an extra meal. You might as well know that now as later," Aunt Daphne informed her.

"How dare a servant be grumpy with her mistress. Papa never would allow such a thing in his house," Eleanor pointed out. "Why don't you fire her?"

"Fire her? Oh, my dear, do you have any notion of how difficult it is to find a good cook? As it is, I have to let her off on Sundays and Thursdays."

"She must have it easy, cooking for one. I'd conjecture that she has the better end of the bargain."

Her aunt flinched. "So you say. But you see, with the advent of your arrival, her duties have doubled."

"True. And speaking of my arrival, I am ready to retire to my quarters, by your leave." Realizing that she still enjoyed the status of a guest, Eleanor tried to keep her voice from sounding too demanding.

"What was I thinking? Of course, you're tired." Aunt Daphne turned slightly and swept her arm toward the foyer. "Your room is upstairs. It's the second door on the right, beside my room."

"Thank you." Eleanor didn't move right away, expecting her aunt to escort her. Instead, Aunt Daphne peered into the gilded wall mirror and brushed her hands over her chignon. Eleanor watched her for a moment until she turned back to face her.

"Well?" Aunt Daphne asked. "Is there a question?"

"No, Aunt Daphne."

"Then unless you didn't learn how to tell right from left at that fancy finishing school that graduated you, I suggest you get situated. For future reference, breakfast is served at six on the dot, luncheon is served at the stroke of noon, and dinner is served at six thirty every night. No exceptions." She nodded once toward the grandfather clock that could be seen from the parlor although it dominated the front hall. "It's already five thirty. I'd best prepare now."

"My, but you are organized." Eleanor wasn't accustomed to such a strict schedule and wondered how she would cope. Unsure of what to do next, she stared at her aunt and discovered she couldn't move one foot in front of the other.

A flash of realization swept over Daphne's face. "You aren't used to doing anything for yourself, are you? I know your father. He spoiled you rotten, I'm sure." Her kind tone belied her biting words. "As you can plainly see, there is no man in this house to see to it that your pretty little slippers never touch a drop of mud on the street. Here, you will find yourself comfortable, but you will also discover that the Kerr women fend for themselves."

"Yes, ma'am." Spurred by her aunt's words, Eleanor finally found the will to travel up the stairs to her room. She would be fending for herself, indeed. She prayed she was up to the challenge.

❧

The following morning, Eleanor watched as Aunt Daphne quickly ate her breakfast. She sat at the head of the dining-room table. After a brief blessing, she tapped the top of her eggshell off and proceeded to dip fingers of toast into the egg, drawing out the runny yolk. Now she was holding the ceramic eggcup with two fingers and spooning out the solid egg white in a ladylike but determined fashion. After sopping up the last of her runny egg with a piece of toast, she still managed to be dainty as she set the tidbit in her mouth.

"This breakfast is delightful." Since she relished runny eggs, Eleanor planned to savor each bite. "And according to our discussions with Cook about the week's menu, there are more good things to come." She allowed herself a tiny smile. Cook's ample figure attested to her skill in the kitchen.

"I'm glad you are finding it agreeable here so far." Aunt Daphne tapped her napkin and quickly set it aside.

"My, what is your hurry, Aunt Daphne?" Eleanor asked.

"Didn't I tell you? We have an appointment today."

"We. . .have. . .an appointment?"

"Of course. With Mrs. Alden."

"Your best patron." Eleanor rose from her seat.

"You remember. Good. In this business, one learns to be accomplished at remembering names. And trust me: Mrs. June Alden is one name you'll want to remember."

"I would think you would be hesitant to return today after yesterday's dispute."

"Oh, that was with Mr. Alden." Aunt Daphne waved her hand in the air as though Mr. Alden were no more than an imaginary bug. "I wouldn't call it a dispute, just part of doing business with them."

Dispute or not, Eleanor felt reluctant. "Why don't you handle it? You don't need me."

"Of course, I need you. You've got to learn the seamstress trade sometime. And there's no time like the present, as they say. Now come along." Aunt Daphne headed toward the foyer. Her heels clicked on the hardwood floors, then were silent when her feet made contact with a rug, then clicked on hardwood once again.

Eleanor knew she was compelled to follow a woman with such a determined pace. By the time she reached the front door, Aunt Daphne had already donned her hat. This time, she wore a crisp white affair with red roses and plumes all around, which matched her white dress embroidered to perfection with red roses.

"My hat!" Eleanor looked down at her morning dress. The beige frock was one of her more sprightly looks, with white lace on the bodice as bold as she dared while in her second stage of mourning. "I'm afraid this won't do."

"Nonsense. Of course, it will do. The color suits you so well." Aunt Daphne sighed. "Sometimes I wish my hair wasn't quite so red. You auburn-haired beauties can wear just about any color you wish and look wonderful."

Eleanor wasn't sure if her aunt was flattering her so she would hurry along, of if her words were sincere. She suspected her words sprouted from a combination of both. "If you insist, I'll wear this."

Aunt Daphne studied her. "You sewed it yourself, didn't you?"

Eleanor nodded. "Of course."

Aunt Daphne fingered the lace on the bodice of Eleanor's dress near her shoulder, then checked the hem of her skirt. Her inspection earned Eleanor a nod. "Very good. This is a fine example of your work. Soon we will double our business."

"Obviously, if we visit our best patrons every day." She couldn't resist a little sardonic smile.

Aunt Daphne laughed. "Mrs. Alden must look at muslin samples today, as she took too long with her lace yesterday. Doing business with her takes longer than with most of my other clients. She tends to delay each process. She does have a companion, a rather dreary girl named Vera Howard, though she is from a good family. Otherwise, Mrs. Alden is a lonely old soul."

Eleanor nodded with understanding.

"Don't forget your sewing basket," her aunt called to Eleanor, who rushed up the stairs.

"I won't," she called back, even though she hadn't thought about it despite the fact they had discussed nothing but sewing for the past few minutes. The idea of being a businesswoman had just begun to take hold of her, and carrying sewing notions with her at all times was merely a beginning.

Father in heaven, I beseech Thee to be with me!

Moments later, Eleanor hurried to the waiting carriage. As she situated herself, Eleanor straightened her hat, a simple mauve invention with a ribbon of lace that matched her dress. She secured her hat with a long stickpin made of ivory.

"I must say, the materials of which your hat is comprised outweigh in quality the imagination of your milliner," Aunt Daphne noted.

"Truly?" Eleanor patted the brim. "I rather like this hat."

Aunt Daphne shrugged. "It's well enough, I suppose. But we must take you to Eva's to have more hats made for you."

Eleanor self-consciously touched the brim of her under-stated hat. She liked her own style and wondered if she could feel comfortable dressing as outrageously as her aunt. "I assume she is your milliner?"

"Yes, and she makes me a hat in exchange for a dress. It's a sweet scheme that lets us both cut a fine figure everywhere we go."

"Eva, Vera, Raleigh Alden, Mrs. Alden—my head is swimming as I try to remember all these names."

"Don't worry. You sound as though you will do just fine. I must admit, remembering Raleigh Alden is easy enough. Every eligible lady in town sees him and swoons on the spot." She sighed. "If only I were a decade younger."

"Aunt Daphne!" Eleanor leaned toward her. "I thought he was a miser."

"He is. And so I shall let him pass by. Not that he has ever made any overtures toward me, really." She looked over her niece. "He's a little older than you are. Just about to see his thirtieth birthday, I'd say."

"My, how you talk." Eager to discourage any potential for matchmaking on her aunt's part, Eleanor deflected the conversation from herself as quickly as she could. "With all this calculation and speculation, am I to assume you are ready for another suitor after all these years?"

"Your father told you." Aunt Daphne's pretty features tight-ened, and her body stiffened.

Her stricken look sent a shot of discomfort through Eleanor. Yet if the two women hoped to live together in peace, she realized she might as well tell her aunt what she knew. She leaned her back against the seat to convey a casual attitude. "Oh, someone mentioned once that you had many suitors, but one in particular stood out among the rest."

Aunt Daphne nodded. "Long ago, when I was young. We courted fifteen years, in fact. Then he met someone else and,

and. . ." Her lips drew together to form a tense contour.

"I know." She took Aunt Daphne's hands in hers. Her aunt's thumb bore a callous from years of working as a seamstress, but otherwise her hands were softer than Eleanor had anticipated. "Obviously, he suffered from a severe lack of judgment."

Aunt Daphne's eyes misted, a sure indication that she had never recovered fully from her heartbreak. Looking down at her hands in Eleanor's, she nodded several times in a rapid motion. "That's what all my friends say."

Eleanor gave her aunt's hands a firm squeeze, then released them. She hadn't imagined she could befriend her spinster aunt, but already she felt a bond with Daphne.

"I do enjoy my freedom," Aunt Daphne observed. "And if I were to marry, most likely my husband would insist that I give up my career."

"You might give up fashioning dresses for wages, but I doubt you would be forced to abandon sewing forever," Eleanor couldn't resist noting. "On the contrary, you might be busier than ever making frocks and bloomers for a brood of little ones."

"At my age?" Aunt Daphne's laughter tinkled throughout the carriage. "I would barely have time for a husband, and the arrival of a baby would be a minor miracle at best."

Eleanor studied her aunt's face. "Maybe you could consider a widower with children."

"Oh, I've had my share of those to come knocking, but who can travel and see the world when one is responsible for someone else's children?"

"Travel?"

"Oh, yes. I would love to travel. That is my dream. To save up enough money to travel the world." Excitement caused her voice to rise in pitch and speed. "Wouldn't you like to take a steamship to Europe someday? Or maybe even see the pyramids in Egypt?" She set her gaze toward the window, staring out it as though she could see the Sphinx just on the horizon rather than the lawn of a fine house they passed.

Eleanor hesitated. "Well, I just did travel across the country." She didn't add that the experience had cured her of any desire to journey anywhere else for the next few months—or years.

Aunt Daphne turned her attention to Eleanor. "Exactly. Wouldn't it be a wonderful idea for the two of us to travel together?" She clasped her hands at the thought.

Eleanor felt the muscles in her chest tighten. "Travel together?"

"Yes. I was hoping that perhaps you'd be keen on the idea of being my traveling companion—and the daughter I always wanted."

Eleanor clinched her hands and rubbed her fingers together. Looking down, she felt her eyes moisten. How could she not be flattered by her aunt's emotions? Then again, how could she tell her aunt that she had no desire to see the world? "I—I haven't thought much about traveling, really. In fact, I've barely had enough interest to observe the sights on this very trip."

"Oh, you'll learn Baltimore soon enough." Aunt Daphne dispatched a pitiable look her way. "I know why your dreams have been so small. You've been so burdened with responsibilities and occupied with tending to your sick mother. *Tragic* is the only way to describe her death. But let's not speak of it now. We must put on a happy demeanor if we are to please Mrs. Alden. Remember, we are there to provide our patrons with happiness, not to trouble them with our concerns."

Eleanor remained silent. Spending long amounts of time in a confined space, whether in a luxurious carriage, a train, or a steamship, held no appeal for her. She couldn't imagine a scenario where she would desire to globetrot. Rather than embracing the world after being confined to her time of mourning, Eleanor had made up her mind to live as a religious solitary. What better way to escape heartbreak and pain in the world? She remembered her mother and wished she could have died in her place. Eleanor knew in her heart that her grief was as strong a reason for Papa's insistence that she relocate as his concern for her physical health. He had seen her rebellion when he insisted she head to the safety of a cooler climate so she, his only child, could remain well and start life anew. But a religious life was not his plan for her and certainly no idea of her aunt's.

No one but Eleanor knew how many nights she had spent in anguished prayer, seeking guidance from her heavenly Father. Despite her pleas to let her live a life alone, she felt no leading in that direction.

"Child," Aunt Daphne said, interrupting her thoughts. "Why are you so pensive?"

Eleanor didn't rush to answer. Clearly, Aunt Daphne had big plans for her. Should she tell all and risk her wrath? Or perhaps if she were honest, Daphne could help her find her calling. She took in a breath and spoke. "I know that Papa has asked you to teach me to be a seamstress, but that is not my wish. Ever since Mama's death, I have been praying for guidance on how I might live life as a religious solitary," she confessed. "I was in hopes that you might have suggestions as to how I might pursue that course here in Baltimore."

"A religious solitary?" Aunt Daphne's laughter echoed throughout the carriage. "Don't be silly, Eleanor. You are much too beautiful to cloister yourself. Your father knows that, and he knows your disposition. We'd better follow his instructions."

"I know that Papa has my best interests at heart, but it is inner beauty I seek."

"And I am sure you possess that in abundance." Aunt

Daphne studied her. "I know you do. You radiate beauty. And our local bachelors will see that soon enough."

Eleanor felt her face flush hot. "I am not interested in a courtship, Aunt Daphne."

"We shall see," Aunt Daphne said as the carriage came to a stop in front of a brick Georgian style house with a spacious lawn. "Here we are. The Alden residence. Your first test will be your meeting with Raleigh Alden, Esquire. Are you ready?"

"More than ready." She lifted her nose in the air, practicing her most snobbish look. She was determined to take on her aunt's challenge and pass her first test.

She would steel herself against any and all winsome bachelors. And that included Raleigh Alden, Esquire.

two

With fear and trepidation, Eleanor stepped out of the carriage. What would Mrs. Alden be like? An image of an aged dowager formed in her mind. She pictured a stout woman dressed in an elaborate silk frock sewn by Aunt Daphne, looking through spectacles down her nose at Eleanor. She shuddered, then walked behind her aunt, assuming her role as apprentice. On the one hand, she wanted nothing more than to hide behind her aunt's skirts. On the other, she hoped she wouldn't prove to be too outspoken once she overcame her initial shyness—an unfortunate trait she longed to master.

At the end of the walk stood a sign posted on a wooden stake, painted in a stodgy black script. RALEIGH ALDEN, ATTORNEY AT LAW. The very existence of the sign lent importance to Raleigh's station.

"His clients have to come a ways to see him, don't they?" Eleanor suggested.

"He always talks about leasing an office in the city, but so far he hasn't." Aunt Daphne shrugged. "I suppose he has plenty of business as it is. He's quite good, you know. Now come along."

The two women headed up the curved brick walk toward the front door.

Eleanor hissed, "Shouldn't we go to the back door?"

Daphne slowed her pace but didn't stop. "We may be seamstresses, but we are not ordinary. Mrs. Alden considers me almost as a friend. We go to the front door."

Eleanor noticed that her aunt lifted her head with a confident air and strode along as though she were equal to the occupants of the streamlined, brick mansion. The arms of two massive oak trees surrounding the house looked as though they were cradling the building. She could imagine surveying such oaks when Caecilius Calvert, second Baron Baltimore, became Maryland's first governor in the seventeenth century. Shaking such silly thoughts out of her mind, she admired the flowers by the stoop and along the front of the house. A sizeable group of healthy gladiolas was in full bloom, obviously tended by an expert gardener.

Aunt Daphne lifted the large brass door knocker and waited. A butler promptly answered. "Good morning, Miss Kerr." He nodded to Eleanor.

"Good morning, Monroe."

"Mrs. Alden is expecting you. You may go up now."

Up? Eleanor wondered what location the butler meant. Why wouldn't they be meeting Mrs. Alden in one of the formal rooms on the first floor?

Aunt Daphne nodded and stepped into a foyer much grander than Eleanor had seen in recent memory. Then again, she had stayed to herself and had had few occasions to visit the truly wealthy back in Louisiana. Without a moment's hesitation, Aunt Daphne glided toward an oversized mahogany staircase. The deeply colored wood contrasted well with the white wallpaper with a gold damask pattern.

"Come along, Eleanor," Aunt Daphne prompted.

Feeling like a small child upon being issued a command, Eleanor flinched but obeyed. She followed her aunt up a curved staircase that five people could have ascended side by side in comfort. When she reached the top, she looked down and noticed that the height was almost dizzying, but somehow the foyer appeared even more imposing from such a vantage point.

The clacking of her aunt's heels warned her not to dawdle. Aunt Daphne led her down an expansive hallway. They passed occasional tables decorated with flowers that were most likely plucked from the formal gardens. Eleanor looked up and noticed that portraits of people from other eras in history flanked the hallway. She presumed the finely attired lords and ladies were Alden ancestors.

She watched her aunt turn into the fourth door on the left.

"You're late," a shrill feminine voice chastised her aunt before her second foot had stepped over the threshold.

Late! Eleanor didn't think so and wondered how her aunt would defend herself.

Eleanor hovered in the hallway, wary of entering the room. As though she could read Eleanor's thoughts, Aunt Daphne sent her a look that commanded her to enter behind her. Eleanor tiptoed over the threshold, hoping she could stay close enough to her aunt so as not to draw attention to herself.

"I beg your indulgence," Aunt Daphne said, displaying a surprising humility that Eleanor hadn't seen from her previously. "There has been some excitement at my house upon the arrival of my niece."

Oh, no! Aunt Daphne wasn't going to let her fade into the wallpaper!

To Eleanor's horror, Daphne stepped aside so Eleanor would come into full view of their patron. "Mrs. Alden, I would like to present my niece, Eleanor Kerr."

The elderly lady was propped up in a bed that was big enough to sleep four in comfort. The headboard was fashioned from a rich brown mahogany embellished with elaborate carving. Eleanor fought the impulse to run her fingers over the smooth wooden dogwood flowers. Despite the heat, Mrs. Alden chose to remain under a thick coverlet of white eyelet lace. Since the woman wore a bed jacket and a high-necked gown of white, Eleanor had trouble discerning where Mrs. Alden ended and the bed sheets began.

Pillows covered in white cotton reminded Eleanor of fluffy

clouds. If Mrs. Alden had held a harp and had wings—and if she hadn't been wearing a white nightcap with gray tendrils of hair peeking out strategically—Eleanor imagined she might have looked like an angel in a Renaissance painting. Eleanor wasn't sure whether to approach Mrs. Alden and shake her hand or curtsy as though the woman were royalty. Remembering Mrs. Alden's importance to her aunt, Eleanor decided to make a motion that would not require her to speak. She curtsied.

"A curtsy!" Mrs. Alden clapped. "How delightful, my dear. It is not often that one of the younger generation is quite so charming."

"She's a Kerr through and through." Pride rang through Aunt Daphne's voice. The reward made Eleanor feel a little less squeamish about her unfamiliar gesture. "I know you won't mind Eleanor's presence here, Mrs. Alden. I'm thinking about allowing her to work with me on a regular basis."

Allowing her to work? Eleanor thought the matter was settled. Maybe she could pursue other dreams, after all.

"What a grand idea. I think she will make a charming addition to your business." Mrs. Alden eyed the far corner of the room. "Perhaps your apprentice could fashion a frock for Vera."

Eleanor snapped her head in the direction where a young woman sat. Apparently she had been observing without making her presence known. Considering that her chignon was of a bland color and her dress a mint green similar to the color of the wall, the feat of blending in was easily accomplished.

"Of course, she would be pleased to fashion a frock for Vera," Aunt Daphne answered for Eleanor. "As you can see, my niece sews a fine seam. She, herself, made the dress she is wearing."

Mrs. Alden crooked her finger toward Eleanor. "Come closer and let me see your handiwork, young lady."

Nervous that she might say or do something that would lower Mrs. Alden's opinion of her—and consequently Aunt Daphne—Eleanor resolved to keep her answers polite but as brief as possible. She obeyed despite suddenly becoming aware of her beating heart. Mrs. Alden wasn't unkind, but she somehow managed to frighten Eleanor all the same.

The old woman leaned closer and stretched out an aged, bony hand sprinkled with brown liver spots. Eleanor tried not to cringe as the old woman fingered the black lace on her dress much as Aunt Daphne had earlier. After such thorough examinations, Eleanor feared the poor little piece of delicate crochet work would soon become ragged with wear.

"Very fine. Very fine, indeed," Mrs. Alden clucked. "Vera?"

Vera rose and approached the bed. "Yes, ma'am?"

"How would you like for Eleanor here to make you a dress?"

"Thank you. But I—I don't have much need for a dress, Mrs. Alden." Vera's voice was as refined as it was shy.

"Stuff and nonsense! Of course, you have need for a dress. How about a new church dress in a nice shade of green to go with your eyes?"

Since Mrs. Alden pointed out the color of Vera's eyes, Eleanor noticed that they were, indeed, a startling shade of green. Vera nodded. "Yes, ma'am. That would be very nice."

"I'm sure Eleanor will have some marvelous ideas for Vera," Aunt Daphne assured Mrs. Alden.

"Good. Perhaps Eleanor can stop by at ten in the morning on Friday for Vera's initial fitting."

"Yes, she can," Aunt Daphne affirmed.

Eleanor wondered how Vera felt about Mrs. Alden speaking for her, determining the time of the fitting and the color and occasion for the dress. Then she realized that she had been permitting her aunt to speak for her as though she were a mute. Eleanor couldn't resist throwing a sympathetic look

Vera's way. Vera cast her eyes downward in return. Eleanor made a mental note not to suggest any shade of hue that was too vibrant, lest the thought overpower such a reticent soul.

"Now, Eleanor," Mrs. Alden said, "Miss Vera Howard is more than a companion to me. She is descended from one of Maryland's finest families. I expect you to take the utmost care with her dress."

"I will, indeed, ma'am."

"Very well."

Eleanor cast her gaze toward the young woman, who sent her a shy smile before returning to her place in the corner.

Since Vera obviously wasn't prepared to talk, Eleanor watched as her aunt showed several muslin and lace samples to her client. Mrs. Alden lingered over each decision as though the garments she was ordering would be her last. To Eleanor's eyes, the nightwear set that Mrs. Alden wore looked elegant. Why she was ordering more was beyond Eleanor's capacity to reason. But who was she to object to any business for her aunt?

Eleanor marveled at how Aunt Daphne skillfully increased Mrs. Alden's initial order from one nightgown to add a bed jacket and nightcap. As she chose one fine sample after another, Eleanor could see that Aunt Daphne was pleased.

"Well, that should serve you quite nicely, Mrs. Alden," Aunt Daphne proclaimed upon the culmination of the order.

"Good. Raleigh is in his office downstairs. He should be finished meeting with his client by now," Mrs. Alden said. "He'll be glad to settle the bill from my last order."

"Yes, ma'am." If Aunt Daphne wanted to throw Eleanor a doubtful look, she resisted the urge. After quickly putting away her samples, she snapped her brown leather bag shut and left the room, motioning with her head for Eleanor to follow her.

Eleanor was starting to feel more and more like a lackey

instead of a woman in charge of her own destiny. She prayed for the strength to remain humble.

She followed Aunt Daphne down the stairs toward the first floor, then to a spacious room in the front of the house. Eleanor wished that Vera hadn't become her first client. Then she wouldn't have to worry about settling any bills with the dreadful Raleigh Alden.

"Maybe I should wait in the carriage," Eleanor whispered.

"No. You'll be making clothes for Vera, so Mr. Alden needs to meet you." Aunt Daphne stopped in front of the door and fumbled through her bag. "I can't find my account ledger. Will you go to the carriage and fetch it for me?"

"Of course." Eleanor was more than happy to delay her meeting with Mr. Alden.

"Don't tarry, and come right into the office."

"I will," Eleanor promised as she heard Aunt Daphne knock on the office door.

"Come in." The masculine southern drawl didn't sound nearly as threatening as Eleanor had imagined it would. In fact, the voice sounded rather melodious and pleasant. Maybe its owner wouldn't be such an ogre after all.

She hurried to the carriage, discovered the book where it had fallen onto the floor, and rushed back to the house as she had promised.

"I just paid you more than ten dollars. What is the meaning of such a large order for today?" The southern drawl had become clipped.

Eleanor stopped near the door, afraid to enter.

"Your mother expressed a need for new clothing, and I intend to fulfill it." Aunt Daphne's voice indicated that she had no notion of relinquishing her order.

"A need! Pshaw!" he objected. "Mother already owns fifteen nightgowns, seven hats, three robes, and five bed jackets."

"How conscientious of you to keep such a close count."

"Mother is getting on in years, and her health is failing. It is my duty as her son to see to it that she is not taken advantage of."

Taken advantage of! Why, how dare he accuse her aunt of trying to take advantage of anyone!

Though she had all but cowered before Mrs. Alden in deference to her age and status, Eleanor felt differently toward this arrogant man. Certainly he was important, but he had no right to treat her aunt in such a way.

She listened for her aunt to defend herself but heard no retort. Eleanor couldn't tolerate the suspense. She had to interrupt and set affairs straight then and there.

Eleanor stepped into the room. Though she shut the door behind her, she kept her hand on the glass doorknob. In her fury, she clutched it as though she were a war ship and the knob her only anchor against a rising tide. Then she noticed Raleigh Alden. She strained to keep from gasping. Aunt Daphne had been right about his handsome features and dashing demeanor. No wonder the women swooned!

Remembering her ire, she composed herself. "Mr. Alden, I'll have you to know that my aunt would never take advantage of anyone! On the contrary, it is you who are robbing your dear mother if you deny her the small pleasure of a few nice garments in which to spend her waning years!" As her anger grew, she felt her body flush.

Only after she finished her speech did she notice a pair of blue eyes that twinkled like stars in the midnight sky. A straight nose led to even straighter teeth.

"Eleanor!" Aunt Daphne cried.

"Well, it's true." She straightened her shoulders. "You would never sell any woman a garment she didn't truly want to wear." She looked squarely at her aunt. "And any woman would be happy to wear clothes fashioned by you, Aunt Daphne. They are among the most exquisite I have ever seen!"

Her rage spent, Eleanor looked at Raleigh. Instead of the anger she expected, his expression seemed open, as though he could burst into laughter if his funny bone were tickled with the lightest touch of a feather.

He glanced at her and seemed to sit a bit straighter, and his face lit with fascination. Eleanor knew she wasn't being vain. Clearly, in spite of her outburst, or perhaps because of it, she had piqued his interest. Suddenly shy, she took a newfound interest in examining the pattern of the red floor runner.

"You speak with great boldness for one who has not been introduced." Raleigh looked at Aunt Daphne as he rose from his seat situated behind a large mahogany desk that had been polished to a mirrorlike finish. "I'm assuming this is the apprentice of whom you spoke?"

Since Raleigh's attention was now on her aunt, Eleanor summoned the courage to observe him. Funny, he didn't look like the cheapskate that her aunt had described. His dark hair was polished to a sheen, the current popular style. His blue seersucker suit was tailored in the latest fashion, and Eleanor could see even from across the room that his tailor had sewn an expert seam. How could a man who dressed himself in such a fine manner object to a bit of lace for his mother?

"Yes. Mr. Raleigh Alden, may I present my niece, Miss Eleanor Kerr. Miss Eleanor Kerr, this is Mr. Raleigh Alden."

"How do you do, Mr. Alden?"

"How do you do?" He nodded, the twinkle still lighting his eyes. "I understand you have an issue to discuss with me?"

"Never mind my niece," Aunt Daphne apologized. "She has been a bit excitable since she's had such a long trip."

"A long trip? From where?"

"Louisiana," Aunt Daphne answered. "The New Orleans area."

"Ah, the land of hanging moss and spicy food." Raleigh folded his arms but looked at her with an expression of renewed interest. "So how do you like Baltimore?"

"I'm afraid I haven't been here long enough to ascertain how I like it. I do know that the weather isn't as cool as I thought it might be."

"Cool in the summer? You would have to move much farther north for that." His voice softened so much that the drawl returned. "Might I offer you a glass of iced tea?"

She didn't want to take a glass of tea from Raleigh, but since he had brought up the subject, she was feeling a bit thirsty. "That might be nice."

"Have a seat." He motioned to the two chairs in front of his desk. "And you, too, of course, Miss Kerr," he said to Aunt Daphne.

Aunt Daphne's eyebrows shot up. "I suppose you might wish to call us Miss Daphne and Miss Eleanor to avoid confusion."

"With your permission." Raleigh picked up a silver bell on his desk and rang for the butler, who promptly appeared at the door.

"Yes, sir?"

"Monroe, deliver us three tall glasses of iced tea."

"Yes, sir." Monroe disappeared.

"Now," Raleigh drawled, "perhaps we might all come to our senses as we drink our tea." He sent a direct look to the elder of the two women. "Miss Daphne, you have been my mother's seamstress for a number of years. Perhaps you are not trying to take advantage of her good nature."

"Of course not." Aunt Daphne sniffed.

"But certainly you can understand why I would question this extravagance."

"The extravagance is hers, not mine, Mr. Alden," Aunt Daphne said. "She chose the finest Irish linen and lace embroidered in Italy for her latest lingerie set."

"With your encouragement, no doubt."

Her encouragement? Was he trying to insinuate that Aunt Daphne insisted that her customers overbuy? Eleanor tightened her lips.

Aunt Daphne didn't hesitate to answer. "I simply showed her all of my samples. She chose the finest because she has a good eye for quality." Aunt Daphne set her hands in her lap.

"And you do as well, sir," Eleanor interrupted, "judging from the tailoring of your fine suit."

"Thank you, but I am a businessman and must dress accordingly."

Eleanor took a moment to observe the office, which appeared much as she had expected. Obviously a legal office would be open to public scrutiny at a moment's notice, and the opulent furnishings and spotless appearance of the room reflected its occupant's esteemed stature. "I can see that you are serious about your business. Shouldn't your mother enjoy some of the fruits of your labor?"

"Of course. . ."

Eleanor felt ire rise inside her with an intensity she hadn't remembered in quite some time. For her aunt's sake, she didn't mind cowering before the lawyer's mother. Although Mrs. Alden seemed high and mighty, she was a worthy client. But the arrogance of her son! It was just too much. Entirely too much.

"I see a Bible on your shelf." Eleanor nodded to a spot behind Raleigh's right shoulder. "The heavenly Father commands us to honor our mothers and our fathers."

"Yes," Raleigh accepted her point.

Monroe entered and placed the tea before them without a sound.

"I honor my mother by making sure that her interests are protected," Raleigh pointed out. "I haven't been here in Baltimore long, having just returned home after living in Tallahassee, Florida, the past ten years. I only returned to care for my ailing mother."

"And if I might say so, I do admire your sacrifice," Eleanor said. "Are you an only child as I am?" She took several swallows of the refreshing liquid.

He guffawed. "Hardly. I have six brothers. All of them have families of their own, however. So I, the youngest by far and a bachelor, took the duty with cheer, for I am fulfilling the Lord's commandment."

"And part of your duty is to see that your mother is well dressed," Aunt Daphne pointed out.

"Not at the prices you're charging."

As if Aunt Daphne could control the cost of fine imported goods!

"I apologize for the increase, but my costs have risen, and you must consider that I have no choice but to pay dearly to import your mother's fabrics." Aunt Daphne took a sip of her tea, a gesture that Eleanor suspected she was using to control her indignation.

"I wish you would not tempt her with the finest textiles. As you know, she is a professional invalid and receives very few visitors. She hardly needs the finery you propose even though she can well afford it."

Despite the cooling effects of the iced tea, Eleanor felt hotter than the July sun. She had no intention of sitting there any longer and listening to this man criticize her aunt, no matter how attractive and well dressed he might be. Against her better judgment, she rose from her seat.

"Mr. Alden, with all due respect, I will not tolerate your insults toward my aunt. Consider our order cancelled."

three

Raleigh tried to compose himself when he heard Eleanor's unexpected proclamation. He stood in deference to the fact that Eleanor had risen from her seat. "Cancelled? You're canceling my mother's order—just like that?" Raleigh snapped his fingers.

"Yes. Just like that."

Raleigh was taken aback. Surely a cancellation would save him money, but now that the threat was at hand, he wasn't sure he wanted the order to be terminated. His mother was certain to be unhappy now that she had selected material, only to find that she wouldn't be receiving her new cap, bed jacket, and gown after all. She always looked forward to receiving her new outfits with great anticipation.

Raleigh didn't know how to respond to the irate young woman standing before him. He knew he should be upset by her behavior, but he enjoyed hearing her educated phrasing executed with a Louisiana drawl. Even though Daphne claimed her niece was overwrought from her recent trip, he had a sneaking suspicion that she was one to speak her mind regardless of the circumstances.

Daphne jumped from her seat with such haste that she nearly spilled the glass of tea she was holding. "Don't listen to her. She hasn't been herself since she lost her dear mother."

For the first time, Raleigh realized that Eleanor's plain dress was edged with the black lace of a woman in the second stages of mourning. A sense of shame overwhelmed him. "Allow me to express my deepest sympathies, Miss Eleanor."

"Thank you." Her voice softened only somewhat.

"She only has another month left before she can return to her normal life," Daphne informed him.

"I know that must be pleasant news for you," Raleigh told Eleanor.

"Yes, although I shall always mourn for my dear mama deep within my heart."

"Of course." He observed that she couldn't have yet seen her twenty-fifth birthday. If so, she would be at least seven years younger than he. A successful lawyer well versed in dealing with people who didn't always want to reveal the truth, the whole truth, and nothing but the truth, Raleigh prided himself on his ability to read faces for signs of intrigue or deception. He searched Eleanor's face for a hint that she referred to her grief in order to make him squirm. He found nothing in her features but sincere emotion. Indeed, he felt like a heel for quarreling over his mother's clothing expenses when Eleanor had no mother at all.

He felt the ladies' eyes upon him as they waited for him to settle the account. He pursed his lips together. After his arrival in Baltimore, Raleigh had not been pleased to discover the untidy state of his mother's financial affairs. Though most of the merchants had treated her with honesty, Raleigh's sharp eyes had spotted several irregular charges to various accounts, and he had spent no small amount of time securing refunds for his aging parent. June Alden had never worried about money and as a result had proven too trusting, leaving her vulnerable to being overcharged for goods she did use or billed for goods she never bought. Surely the Kerrs were too smart to begin such a practice now that he had taken charge of his mother's affairs. But for her sake, he had to question them.

"I realize that taking on the employ of your niece has resulted in an increase in your expenses," he told Daphne. "I do hope my mother will find her services of enough value to justify this propagation in price."

"Wait," Eleanor protested. "I am an expert seamstress in my own right, and I plan to be an asset to my aunt's business. As for the increase, I had no idea that her price was going up until she told you herself."

"While I do not approve of my niece's outburst, she does speak the truth," Daphne assured him.

"Very well," he said. "But do not think for a moment that my mother's orders alone can support your business."

"We never would think such a thing." Insult colored Daphne's voice. "I have plenty of clients to keep me busy."

"But not all of them are as wealthy as my mother," Raleigh pointed out.

"Perhaps not, but they do pay their bills without a fuss." Daphne's mouth straightened itself into a firm line, and her steady gaze met his without flinching.

Her meaning wasn't lost on Raleigh. Perhaps he wasn't showing his best manners in being so difficult about settling his mother's bill, however extravagant.

Raleigh looked at Eleanor with a more discerning eye. She was a beauty, for certain. Eleanor was far more pleasing to the eye than her aunt, and Daphne Kerr had been a known beauty in her day. Though he guessed she had passed her fortieth birthday, remnants of her former glory were evident on her still-youthful face. He studied the younger Kerr woman for a second time. How could he not admire Eleanor, a woman of such courage and conviction—a woman who was willing to risk losing a client to defend her aunt?

He opened his lips. "You're right."

Eleanor's brown eyes lit, and her mouth dropped open. "I am?" Just as quickly, she shut her lips. "I mean, I know I'm right. Of course, I'm right."

Raleigh suppressed an amused look. So she didn't think she

would win the battle she had so bravely waged. Had her emotions overcome her common sense? Or was she merely courageous to a fault? Either idea intrigued him.

Eleanor straightened her narrow shoulders. "I'm glad you see the sensibleness of my position, Mr. Alden."

"Indeed, I do." Raleigh turned his face to Daphne. "I wouldn't like for my clients to argue over my fees, and I should show you—and your niece—the same courtesy. Forgive me."

"I—I, of course."

"I will settle my mother's bill in a timely manner." He returned to his desk, sat down in the brown leather armchair, and reached for his fountain pen and book of blank bank drafts. "How much do you need today, Miss Kerr?"

For the first time, Daphne appeared flustered. "Fifty percent, as always." He watched as she searched her papers. She found an itemized statement written on lined paper and handed it to him. "With the rest payable upon delivery of the garments. If that is agreeable to you."

He looked over the charges. A deposit of twenty dollars seemed a bit extravagant for a night set, but Raleigh nodded and proceeded to make out the draft. Perhaps the amount was in reality not unreasonable at all. Raleigh knew that his mother was purchasing more than a nightgown. She was buying a bit of companionship and interaction with her seamstress. Why else would she permit Daphne to saunter up the front walk as though she owned the place?

He supposed that even though they paid Vera Howard handsomely, the young woman was barely beyond her teen years and could only provide so much conversation, cooped up as she was with his mother.

Raleigh handed Daphne the bank draft. "There you are. I give you this deposit in good faith." He looked over at Eleanor. "I expect you to sew the fine seam you promised."

"Oh, but I will be sewing your mother's gown, Mr. Alden,"

Daphne said. "Eleanor will be fashioning one for Miss Howard."

"Pity." Pity? Had he spoken aloud? Raleigh kept his eyes on the bank draft book as he returned it to the top drawer of his desk.

"Pity?" Daphne's voice betrayed her surprise.

He searched for a rapid recovery and composed himself enough to look at her without wavering. "As you are no doubt aware, my mother is a kind but strict taskmistress. She would teach your niece well how to please even the most discerning patron."

"True." A shadow of a smile kindled itself upon Daphne's face.

Raleigh pictured Vera, his mother's unobtrusive blond companion. Fine frocks would be wasted upon her slight frame. "Who ordered the dress for Miss Howard?"

"Your mother," Daphne responded without missing a beat as she completed her entries in her account ledger.

"Oh." He wondered why but simply smiled at the women and rose from his seat. "Thank you, ladies. I bid you both a good day."

After the required pleasant responses, he watched the two women retreat. Both of them held their heads up, but Eleanor's footfalls were heavy with defiance.

Since her back was to him, Raleigh allowed a grin to impress itself upon his lips. Despite his protests, he couldn't help but anticipate the occasion when he might once again see the beautiful Miss Eleanor Kerr.

❧

"Well," Aunt Daphne noted moments later as they got into their waiting carriage, "I do believe that was the easiest time I've had collecting from Raleigh Alden since he arrived here from Florida."

Eleanor positioned herself in the space beside her aunt.

"The easiest time? Then you must have needed a bullwhip to collect in the past! The nerve of that man. He is as awful as you said. Even worse!"

Daphne positioned herself in her seat, the overpowering, sweet scent of lily of the valley toilette water escaping from the folds of her dress as she adjusted the fabric. "So you believe me now?"

Eleanor felt herself flush. "I never said I didn't believe you."

Aunt Daphne harrumphed and withdrew her fan, swishing it back and forth to cool her face.

Though the carriage had already begun to move, the motion resulted in no relief from the heat. Wilting in the hot air, Eleanor followed her aunt's example and began fanning herself. Less nervous now that the encounter with the Aldens had concluded, she could relax enough to observe the sights they passed. Grand houses stood on large green lawns, houses she could only hope to enter as a seamstress, never as a guest.

A twinge of envy shot through her. Her conscience offered a quick retort.

"For what is a man profited, if he shall gain the whole world, and lose his own soul?" The words from the book of Matthew rang through her head.

A thought occurred to her. "Aunt Daphne? Do you know the people who live in these grand houses?"

Her aunt peered at the particular house they were passing on Dumbarton Road. "That's the Marshall place. Mrs. Alden said that the original owner built it right after the War Between the States." She tilted her head toward a federal style home surrounded by tall oaks. "The Harrisons live there."

"And you know all of them personally?"

"Not all of them. But I suppose at least half the people who live along this road are my patrons." Aunt Daphne sat back in her seat and gave a little smile.

"Do you think they know the Lord?"

"Do they know the Lord? Whatever makes you ask such a thing?" Arched eyebrows and an increased speed in waving her fan told Eleanor that her question puzzled her aunt.

"I just wondered. That's all." Her voice was soft.

"Well, I do know they go to church. Isn't that enough?"

"Not according to scripture. I suppose almost every respectable person goes to church at least some of the time. You have to want to know and love the Lord. To have a relationship with Him."

"That's all well and good, but we can't take on new clients based on how they feel about the Lord," Aunt Daphne advised. "We're in the business of sewing fine dresses for elegant people, not mending their souls."

"I suppose."

"When you work with the public, as we do, you can't be judgmental and stay in business for long."

Eleanor stared at her boots.

"If it makes you feel better, I'll have you know that I've sewn a few church dresses in my time."

Eleanor let out a forced laugh. "I'm sure you have."

"Now, I don't want you conflicting my clients with religious questions." She leaned toward Eleanor. "Do you understand me?"

"But the harvest is rich, and there are so few harvesters."

"You're not going to use Baltimore as a mission field and especially not through my business."

"I'll try to be careful."

"I hope you do a better job of that than you did today. Your papa wrote me and described you as a shy and retiring girl. Clearly, he misinformed me."

"He didn't misinform you, at least not intentionally. I am not quite as outspoken in his company. He is my father, and the Lord commands that I honor him. And he has earned my respect so that even if he weren't my father, I would hold him in the highest regard."

"I'm not surprised to learn of your feelings. I think highly of him as my brother." Aunt Daphne tapped her gloved fingers on the top of her fabric sample case. "So tell me, why did you stand up to him?"

"To Mr. Alden?"

"Yes."

Eleanor stalled. "I—I didn't like the way he was treating you." Just outside of the window were sturdy row houses, a sign they were nearing their part of the city.

Aunt Daphne patted her on the knee. "I've been in business for years and have dealt with all kinds of people. I assure you, I can take care of myself."

"I know, but—"

"But nothing. Don't you realize that you almost lost a large order? And not just any order, but a significant request from an important client. I only hope that you won't make such a grand and foolish gesture again by trying to terminate a sale."

"But you said yourself that you have plenty of clients."

"Yes, but not so many that I can terminate one a day and still hope to maintain my business. I don't think you realize the cost of keeping a house on one's own."

"No, I'm sure I don't."

"Well, you had better acclimate yourself to the idea. You're not in Louisiana anymore. Your papa isn't here to bail you out of trouble."

"Maybe I should go back, then."

Aunt Daphne sighed. "Really, Eleanor, you must learn to make your way in this world. The first item on the agenda is to discard this dangerous habit of making rash proclamations. You must think before you speak. This is a business, not a social or religious endeavor."

"If I could be a religious solitary, I wouldn't have to speak at all. I could just pray all day."

Aunt Daphne let out a hearty laugh that filled the coach. "Where did you get such an idea?"

"From a book," Eleanor admitted. "It was about a woman who lost the love of her life—a sailor who was killed in a shipwreck. She cloistered herself and spent the rest of her days in sweet solitude and prayed for all the ships at sea whenever there was a storm." She sighed. "So romantic."

"Romantic, indeed." Aunt Daphne sniffed. "I'll see to it that you're far too busy here to waste your time with those awful dime novels." She lifted her hands with a motion that showed her disgust and let them fall back on her lap. "A young woman like you in the real world needs to be much more resourceful than a silly little fictional character like that."

"She wasn't silly. She was daring for taking such a vow."

"Perhaps she was, but I can judge by your behavior today that you, my dear niece, wouldn't last a minute. Why, I'd venture a guess that you couldn't even pray in silence for more than half an hour at best."

Eleanor fiddled with the tip of her parasol and wished that she could prove her aunt wrong. But alas, she knew she couldn't.

In fact, judging from her outburst that day, she couldn't hold a civil tongue in her head for long, at least not when the time arose to defend family members. She remembered Raleigh's expression—a combination of surprise and amusement—when she spoke out of turn. Surely her outburst had lowered his opinion of her. Not only must he think her to be an opportunist, but also her tantrum was hardly becoming of a lady—and certainly not a Christian woman.

How could she prove him wrong on both counts?

Even worse, why did she care? The realization struck her that she hadn't bothered about what any man thought of her—not in quite a long while. Perhaps not ever. Her time of courtship had hardly blossomed before her mother took ill, and Eleanor had wanted nothing more than to be near her. Then her period of mourning precluded any opportunity to pique the interest of the local eligible bachelors. Not that she would have been in any frame of mind to entertain suitors even if society hadn't frowned upon such a practice for a woman grieving over the loss of her mother.

Eleanor cut her glance to her aunt. Dressed in such a flamboyant style and color, Daphne was nothing like Eleanor's mother had been. A grand lady in style, though not in position, Mother had spurned embellishments on her clothes and had favored fabrics dyed in hues of cream or a whisper of pink. Her soft-spoken ways reflected her deep and spiritual personality. Admiring her mother, Eleanor had imitated her manners as much as her own fiery personality permitted, obviously with limited success.

Lord, she prayed silently, *I have only been here a half day, and already I have shown myself to be a failure. A dismal failure. Help me!*

❧

Raleigh skimmed a legal brief and laid it aside. The case was routine, a fact that didn't help him concentrate on his work. Images of Eleanor, the beautiful new seamstress with big brown eyes, popped into his head with relentless regularity.

Raleigh had become all too aware since his return to Baltimore that any number of eligible ladies considered him a desirable suitor. Ladies who lived in fine homes, who were born into Baltimore's best families. Why, then, had none of them interested him enough to begin a courtship in earnest? Why was his longing for love piqued only by the auburn-haired seamstress from out of state?

He chuckled as he recalled Eleanor's fine defense of her aunt. He admired her command of language and her passion in its use. His admiration stemmed not just from his professional experiences, but also from his position in society.

Dressed as she had been in the muted hues of the second stage of mourning, Eleanor Kerr hadn't appeared to be one to show such spirit. He wondered what she would be like once she returned fully to life.

Though Baltimore was the town of his boyhood, the city felt alien after he had been so long among the tropical climate and more relaxed attitude of Florida's capital, a place he had grown to love. He had been to Louisiana once to visit an uncle who had made good in New Orleans. The hanging moss on the trees, the warm waters of the Gulf of Mexico, the ebb and flow of the mighty Mississippi River—he could understand why she would miss such a place.

He and Eleanor were both the proverbial fishes out of water. Yes, that was it. That was all that explained his odd attraction to her. A bonding of sorts, the type of emotion that two passengers might share as they trekked across the country together on a train or across the ocean on a transatlantic steamship voyage.

Yes. That was it. That was all. The initial fluttering of his heart would soon still, just as surely as a train would arrive at the next station and as surely as a ship would dock at the next port.

The sound of a tinkling bell interrupted his musings. He sighed and waited.

"Raleigh!"

Mother. Ever so predictable. Within the first few days of his homecoming, he had become acquainted with her routine. Each day flowed into the next with barely a ripple of change.

"Yes, Mother." He rose from his seat and hurried up the stairs. Soon he entered her room and positioned himself a few paces from the foot of the massive bed where she spent most of her time. "What can I do for you, Mother?"

"I understand there was some disagreement over my bill."

"Who told you that?"

She lifted her nose ever so slightly. "Never mind who told me."

Raleigh tightened his lips but remained silent. No doubt one of Mother's loyal servants, most likely Monroe, had rushed to inform her of the afternoon's argument.

She peered down her nose at him. The gesture reminded him of when he was a little boy and she wanted him to confess that he was the ringleader of his group of friends who broke into the abandoned Nash place to explore for hidden treasure. Experiencing the extent of her ire hadn't been worth the expedition's findings—nothing but accumulated filth and the occasional nonhuman resident.

"Did you give Daphne her deposit?" she asked.

"Yes, ma'am."

"Good. I don't want you to dispute her charges anymore. I won't have it said about town that the Aldens are worried about money."

He weighed his next words, careful to maintain the tone of proper respect she deserved. "And I don't want it said about town that you are an innocent and generous lady waiting to be swindled."

"I've known Daphne ever since she opened up shop. She would never swindle me."

"Not intentionally, I'm sure. But her rates have gone up with the arrival of her new apprentice."

"What is your opinion of her new apprentice, Raleigh?" Vera asked.

He snapped his head in the direction of the corner where Vera had set up permanent residence. His opinion? How could he respond?

"I'm interested in the answer to that question as well," Mother prompted. "Did you find her disagreeable? Is that why you quarreled about the bill?"

"No, no," he assured them. What could he say about Eleanor? That he already found her intriguing? No, he couldn't admit that. Never.

"Well?" Mother asked.

"Uh, well. I haven't had time to form an opinion about the niece. I can only assume that if she is a family and business relation of a person you trust, she is respectable enough." He let his gaze bore into Vera since she had first posed the query. What possessed her to ask such a question? Why would she care one way or the other about his opinion of the new seamstress?

Vera nodded and looked down at her lap, where her delicate hands were clasped.

"Why do you ask?" he couldn't resist inquiring. "Is there some concern about her that you need to express?"

"Oh, no. No. Not really. I just wondered what your opinion was. After all, she will be sewing my dresses."

"Is that so?" Raleigh turned his attention to his mother. "I understand that was your idea."

"Yes. She would never ask."

"No, not at all," Vera chirped.

"She hasn't ordered a dress sewn since the cotillion, and I think the time has come for her to have a new frock. You know how careful our Vera is with a dollar," Mother pointed out. "She would never be as extravagant as you accuse me of being."

His mother's unspoken messages were evident to Raleigh. More than once she had hinted that she wouldn't be opposed to his making a match with Vera, an impoverished yet high-born young woman. Even though he felt not the least bit of attraction to Vera, who tended to disappear into the wallpaper, he saw no reason to be unkind. "Yes, I do admire Vera's fortitude."

"You do?" Vera's plain face lit up.

"Uh, yes." He kept his voice even. It was one thing to be kind, but quite another to offer false encouragement. He supposed that if he were to be entirely truthful, he could point out that

Vera was being paid more than enough money to purchase her own dresses; but since his mother wanted to offer her companion a gift, so be it. But why?

"Vera needs a fine dress for the party we'll soon be hosting," Mother said, answering his unspoken question as though she had read his mind.

"Party? I see no reason for a party."

"For your homecoming, of course. Certainly, it is a cause for celebration. I was thinking we could invite a hundred of our close friends."

Raleigh calculated the cost of food and entertainment for such an extravaganza. "There really is no need for all that."

"Oh, certainly there is." She paused. "Or at least a small dinner party."

Raleigh had already learned his mother's tactic of introducing one ridiculous idea before telling him her real intent. "Perhaps that can be arranged."

"I can start helping Mrs. Alden make plans right away," Vera offered.

"Yes, you do that," Raleigh answered, knowing his voice held no enthusiasm. "But Vera, I want you to know that if you don't wish for Eleanor Kerr to be your seamstress, you don't have to feel obligated to her."

"Really?"

"Of course not. I'm sure Daphne would be glad to sew your garment."

"Oh, that's quite all right. I think I can get along with Eleanor well enough. Thank you for your consideration." She blushed and looked back down at her hands.

As Raleigh exited the room, a sense of nervousness overcame him. He wasn't sure what the women were planning for the party, but he had a feeling those plans involved him—and a future he had no intention of living.

four

A few days later, Raleigh had just returned home from a grueling morning in Judge Ross's court when he spied Eleanor walking toward his house. Suddenly feeling chipper despite the fact that the Lord had chosen that day to water the flowers with a light rain, Raleigh hurried his step to meet her—although not too quickly, he hoped.

"Good afternoon, Miss Eleanor," Raleigh greeted her as soon as she was within comfortable earshot. He tipped his hat but not enough to lose the protection it offered from the rain.

She peered at him from underneath her open umbrella. "Good afternoon, Mr. Alden."

He watched the weeping sky. "A lovely day, is it not?"

She looked upward, and when she laughed, the sound reminded him of a tuneful flute. "A lovely day, indeed, if you like gray."

"Gray can be a fine color in its place." He chuckled. "So, what brings you here today?"

"I have an appointment to discuss dress patterns and fabrics with Miss Vera," Eleanor answered as she ascended the verandah steps.

He took her by the elbow, a gesture she didn't seem to mind in the least. For the first time, he felt pleased that his mother had ordered a dress for Vera.

They both stepped onto the verandah. Eleanor shook her wet umbrella with firm but delicate motions. Raleigh opened the door for her. "I trust your aunt is well?"

Eleanor's features became as dark as the day. "Regrettably, she is indisposed with a cold."

45

"Yes, this is a season for such ailments." As he removed his hat and placed it on the mahogany stand in the entrance, Raleigh noted how the house had developed a dank odor as the wood absorbed dampness but couldn't release it back into the heavy atmosphere. He wondered if there was an end in sight to the wet weather.

Monroe, alert as always, had placed a portion of yesterday's newspaper underneath the stand in anticipation of Mr. Alden's dripping hat. "I am so sorry to hear that your aunt has succumbed to illness," Raleigh said. "Please send her my good wishes for her recovery."

"I will." Eleanor deposited her folded umbrella in to a brass stand beside the door. "She will be grateful for your good wishes, I'm sure. She is trying to bring solace to herself by reading."

Raleigh looked around for Monroe, who had not made himself available. He extended his hands in silent offer to take Eleanor's wrap.

After setting down her seamstress's box, she swept herself out of her ivory-colored cloak and handed it to him. "Thank you."

Raleigh nodded. "I'm glad to hear she is reading. Immersion in a good book is one of my favorite pastimes. And I have an extensive library to prove it."

"You seem quite proud of that."

"I suppose I am," he admitted as he shed his overcoat. "Are you a reader?"

"Yes." She looked at the floor. He wondered if her sudden unwillingness to meet his eyes was borne out of modesty or fear of his judgment of her tastes.

"Perhaps you would like to expand your horizons. I could lend you a book," he suggested.

She looked up into his eyes. "You would do that? For me?"

"If it pleases you." He smiled and hoped his expression

didn't reveal that he had an ulterior motive. If he loaned her an expensive volume, she would feel obliged to return it. The transaction would offer him an excuse to see her again and to enter into a lively discussion about what she enjoyed reading. "What subjects interest you?"

She averted her eyes once more. "Oh, I read stories. But my aunt doesn't care for the stories I select."

"To each his own, I say. Why should she criticize you?"

Her face flushed from a creamy buff to a most flattering shade of pink. "I always read scripture to Mama while she was suffering so. The words comforted her. But when she was asleep, I took my mind off my troubles by reading dime novels."

"Oh." No wonder Daphne didn't care for Eleanor's stories. Dime novels hardly offered a young woman the type of intellectual stimulation she needed. Despite siding with her aunt, he decided to encourage her rather than alienate her. "Tell me about your favorite story."

To his surprise, she didn't pause to consider. "My favorite inspired me to pursue the life of a religious solitary."

"A religious solitary?" Experienced in concealing emotions from years of pleading legal cases, he summoned all his expertise to keep from laughing aloud.

"Yes. No one seems to think I would be much of a success at it. Not Papa. Not Aunt Daphne. And I can see by your expression, not even you."

So his act of concealment hadn't been successful! He pursed his lips, then spoke. "I thought Mother mentioned that your aunt attends Lovely Lane Church. Don't you worship with her?"

"Indeed, I do."

"Well." He chuckled. "According to my reading, your spiritual tradition encourages going out among the poor and reaching out to society rather than confining yourself to solitude."

Her eyes studied the fresh arrangement of pink roses that

sat upon an occasional table, yet he could tell by her intense expression that she saw not the flowers but was peering into the doubts in her mind.

"Perhaps," she finally agreed. "But I do believe there is room for different types of religious expression within the confines of the Christian faith, as long as they are scriptural."

Her thoughtful answer impressed him. "You have a good point, indeed. Nevertheless, I have difficulty picturing you wasting away in a dark hole, praying all day and night."

"That's what everyone says, although for the Christian, prayer is never a waste."

He was increasingly impressed by her quick wit. "Yet another point well taken."

She sighed. "I suppose I tend to blurt out what I feel and believe before considering the consequences."

"There, there. Don't become discouraged. The Lord can use any personality to serve Him."

"Do you really think so?" Her eyes lit with hope.

"Indeed, I do." He made a mental search of the books on his library shelves with the intent of making a recommendation. "Perhaps I can suggest a book written in the Middle Ages that may give you some insight. *The Imitation of Christ*. Would you care to borrow it?"

"The Middle Ages?" She hesitated. "I don't know. Is the book terribly long and hard to read?"

This time he held his amusement to himself. "Not terribly on either count. And the chapters are all very short. Like devotional reading. You can peruse a chapter a day in addition to your current spiritual readings without finding it a burden."

"Well, I suppose if you suggest that I should read such a book, I would find the time spent to my benefit. If you wish to loan me your copy, I accept with gratitude. And I promise to take care of, with my best efforts, any book you entrust to me and to return it as soon as I have completed it."

"I'm sure you will. Otherwise, I would not have offered to entrust you with a book from my personal collection." He noticed that Monroe was approaching from the back hallway.

"Good afternoon, Mr. Raleigh." Monroe kept his eyes on Raleigh.

"Afternoon, Monroe."

"I beg your forgiveness for my delay. There was a problem in the kitchen. But all is well now, let me hasten to assure you."

"Of course," Raleigh agreed.

Monroe shot a mean look toward Eleanor. "Is this seamstress disrupting you, sir?" Raleigh noted his disdain as he lingered on the word seamstress.

"Not at all, Monroe. We have been partaking in a rather lively discussion," Raleigh said. "Rather, I am more likely to be disrupting her day."

"Not at all, Mr. Alden," she assured him.

Raleigh flashed Eleanor a smile before returning his attention to Monroe. "Will you escort Miss Kerr to Mother's room?"

"Of course, sir." While Monroe was obsequious toward Raleigh, his glance sent in Eleanor's direction chilled the foyer. Raleigh thought he knew why. More than likely, Monroe questioned the station that Mrs. Alden ascribed to the Kerrs as more than ordinary seamstresses. Daphne and Mrs. Alden had a special bond that no doubt would soon extend to Eleanor.

"If you can abide the interruption to your work, Miss Kerr," Raleigh said, "I can bring the book up to you as soon as I retrieve it from the library."

She paused in midstep. "Are you sure that wouldn't be too much of a bother, Mr. Alden?"

"Please. Call me Raleigh." As soon as the words left his lips, he felt Monroe's gaze boring into him. "And no, it wouldn't be a bother at all."

Her face lit as brightly as the sun illuminating the morning sky. "Thank you."

Raleigh concentrated on her face, deliberately ignoring Monroe. "I'll retrieve the copy for you as soon as possible."

"Thank you."

Her uplifted lips turned into an unhappy straight line. He could see that she felt a twinge of disappointment in that he hadn't invited her to join him. He could understand why. An avid reader, Raleigh enjoyed the mere sensation of being in a library, private or public. The musky odor of leather-bound volumes comprised of fine paper, the room dimly lit to protect valuable tomes, oversized chairs that invited one to sit and linger, stillness that encouraged study—he forced himself to suppress a sigh at the thought. Her unexpressed disappointment pleased him. Surely she was proving herself to be a kindred spirit.

One day, he would feel free to invite her to while away as much time as she liked amid his book collection. But for now, he wanted to conduct himself as a gentleman. No need to fuel the fires of gossip among nosy servants. Private moments between unmarried men and women were not appropriate, even though the new century had dawned. Sometimes he wished convention wasn't quite such a strict taskmistress.

೫

"If you will follow me, Miss Kerr," Monroe offered as soon as Raleigh left them.

Eleanor nodded and climbed the stairs, following Monroe's lead. If only she could have asked Raleigh Alden to let her peek into his library. Obviously, he was proud of his collection of books. Why shouldn't he be able to show them off, even if only to his mother's seamstress?

She straightened herself as she approached Mrs. Alden's door. The pungent smell of liniment would have led her to the right entrance even if Monroe had not.

"Miss Eleanor Kerr to see Miss Howard," Monroe informed the ladies.

Mrs. Alden's voice floated into the hallway. "Oh, good. Do send her in."

Monroe stepped back, never allowing the stern look to leave his features.

Eleanor did her best to ignore him as she stepped over the threshold with warm greetings for the ladies.

"Monroe," Mrs. Alden called before he left her earshot, "please bring us a spot of tea."

"Yes, I shall bring you and Miss Vera tea," he agreed.

"And a cup for Eleanor, too."

Eleanor protested, "Oh, I couldn't—"

"Nonsense. If I am feeling a chill, then you must be, too. Of course, you'll have tea with us."

"Yes, ma'am. It would be an honor." Eleanor didn't dare look at Monroe. She could only imagine how displeased he was with this new development.

She noticed that, as usual, Vera sat in her white satin vanity chair. Eleanor wondered if she ever ventured out of her place. Mrs. Alden was wrapped in white, looking like an aged cherub with smooth skin and hair, which she insisted was prematurely gray. Both women had expressions of anticipation on their faces. Their gazes followed Eleanor's every move.

She searched the room for a spare seat and eyed a wooden chair that matched an oak vanity table. She nodded toward it. "May I?"

"Certainly," Mrs. Alden said.

Eleanor sat her box of sewing notions upon the chair, opened it, and withdrew a few swatches of fabric and a measuring tape. "I hope you like the fabric samples I selected. Aunt Daphne made several excellent suggestions."

"Then I'm sure we'll be delighted," Mrs. Alden said. "We want something quite fancy, something that will make our

Vera shine at the dinner party."

Eleanor looked to Vera for further input, but the young woman just stared at the swatches as though the colors mesmerized her. "All right, then," Eleanor said. "How about green to match your eyes? I also brought a swatch of a particularly nice blue. Or perhaps red?"

"Red?" Vera fanned herself. "Red would never do for a lady."

Eleanor flushed, imagining her face must have looked as red as the silk she held in her hand. "I beg your pardon. I was thinking it was cheerful, that's all."

"She meant no harm, surely," Mrs. Alden said. "I favor the blue."

"Before you decide, I have more selections." Eleanor held two swatches of fabric—one yellow and one blue—to Vera's cheeks. "Both of these are nice, but I do believe yellow brings out the golden highlights in your hair. Very flattering."

"Yellow? That is oh so bright!" Vera squirmed. "Oh, do you really think I should be so daring? I don't want the gentlemen there to think I'm making too extraordinary of an effort to attract their attention."

"No one will think that," Eleanor assured her. From the corner of her eye, she saw Monroe arrive with the tea. "They will just think you're beautiful, that's all."

She put away the swatches. "We'll measure after tea, perhaps?"

"A grand idea," Mrs. Alden agreed.

Vera kept her gaze on her lap, a gesture Eleanor took as shyness.

"You have a fine figure," Eleanor assured her. "I'll find it easy to sew for you."

"Really? You truly think so?"

"Of course, I do." Eleanor wondered why a young woman from such a good family would care what she thought of her. Yet Eleanor found Vera's questions endearing.

"I can't wait to see the dress when it's finished." Vera's enthusiasm reminded Eleanor of a little girl awaiting a birthday celebration.

"I promise to do my best work for you," Eleanor assured her.

"I'm sure any dress you sew will be beautiful, since you are Daphne's niece."

"I'd like to think my sewing is superb, but I confess that I never imagined I would make a living as a seamstress."

"Really? What did you think you would do?"

"I—" She almost said "become a religious solitary," but since she had arrived in Baltimore, she had been told time and again not to nurse such a notion. "I don't know, really. I suppose before Mama died, I thought I would marry and live happily ever after. But she fell ill, and—and. . ." Tears threatened.

"There, there." Vera patted her hand. "God has a plan for everyone. You'll find out what He has in mind for you soon enough."

"I do hope so," Eleanor said, taking a sip of tea.

"In the meanwhile, you'd best bloom where you're planted," Mrs. Alden advised.

"Bloom where I'm planted?"

She nodded. "That means, sew the finest line of stitching you can while you're a seamstress. The job may not seem like His bidding now, but you never know where it might lead." Mrs. Alden tilted her head toward Vera. "Just like my girl, here. One never knows what might occur at this dinner party. Once she's dressed in finery, as she should be, she might get noticed by someone special."

Vera blushed crimson once again. "Oh, Mrs. Alden, how you do talk."

"Do you have anyone in particular in mind?" Eleanor couldn't help but ask.

"No. No one." Vera's adamant shaking of her head told Eleanor otherwise. Her curiosity was piqued, but she knew better than to ask.

"We shall have many fine gentlemen present." Mrs. Alden clasped her hands in obvious rapt anticipation. "Perhaps even Flint Jarvis."

"Flint Jarvis?" Vera gasped.

Eleanor stopped stirring her tea long enough to observe the exchange. The name meant nothing to her, but apparently he was of some repute about town. Aunt Daphne had told her that as a new businesswoman, Eleanor would need to keep her eyes and ears open. Perhaps this bit of gossip was her first test.

"Oh, you can't possibly invite him!" Vera continued.

"Indeed, I can and I will! He is certain to add interest and mystery to any event he attends," Mrs. Alden said. "And no one can deny that he would certainly be a handsome addition to my dinner table."

"Handsome, yes. But with all due respect, do you really think Mr. Alden will get along with someone rumored to be a man about town?" Vera asked.

"Oh, Flint and Raleigh are great friends. And of course, he is my friend Jessica's nephew. Raleigh won't mind at all."

"But what lady shall we invite for Mr. Jarvis?"

Mrs. Alden crossed her arms. "I haven't thought that far ahead yet. But I shall think of someone, I'm sure. We still have time."

"Indeed." Vera shut her mouth and fanned herself as though a burst of heat had entered the room. Since silence penetrated, Eleanor decided that if she was to find out more about the mysterious Mr. Jarvis, the time would be later rather than at the present moment.

"Shall we select a dress pattern?" Eleanor asked.

Vera clapped her hands. "Oh, yes, let's!"

Eleanor couldn't suppress a smile. She didn't remember ever seeing Vera so animated. Certainly the poor girl hadn't had a new dress sewn in ages—or was the prospect of romance more to her liking?

"How about this?" Eleanor showed Vera a picture of a lace-embellished ball gown that was modest yet form-fitting.

"Oh, that's much too bold," Vera said.

Mrs. Alden took the picture out of Eleanor's hand and examined the picture for herself. "Bold? No, I think this is just right."

Vera thumbed through the other patterns that Eleanor had brought. "I was thinking something more along these lines." She showed Mrs. Alden a high-necked dress with full proportions.

"Where will he find you amid all that fabric?"

"I could amend the pattern to suit," Eleanor hastened to offer.

Mrs. Alden studied the picture. "Well, I suppose a nip here and a tuck there." She paused. "As long as Vera's fine figure is evident."

"An easily accomplished feat," Eleanor assured them both.

As the afternoon progressed, Eleanor found that Mrs. Alden agreed with her ideas. She drank her tea as Vera expressed her concern that the dress not be too revealing. Assuring her that it wouldn't, Eleanor packed her box after completing her tea, then took her leave.

She let out a tuneful whistle as she went down the stairs, then remembered that such a feat was hardly ladylike. Yet apparently her tune had caught the attention of Raleigh Alden, since he was standing at the bottom of the stairs. She had been so wrapped up in helping Vera choose her fabric and pattern that she had almost forgotten his promise to bring her a book. Was he waiting to meet her? Eleanor's heart skipped a beat.

"Leaving already, Miss Eleanor?"

"Yes, my appointment went well."

His smile lit the room. "I hope Mother wasn't too difficult."

"Oh, no. Not at all," Eleanor hastened to assure him.

"I beg your pardon for not bringing the book up to you as I promised. I was interrupted by a client," he explained. "So if you have a moment now, would you like to see my library?"

"Yes, I would." She glanced at the grandfather clock in the parlor and noted the time. "My livery isn't due to arrive for another quarter hour."

"Next time, allow me to send my coach," he suggested as they walked side by side through the hallway.

"Oh, I couldn't bother you—"

"Of course. It's no bother. I insist."

Eleanor hadn't expected Raleigh to be so friendly. She had been warned that men who were too sociable too soon might be looking for favors beyond what would be advisable for her to grant. Yet nothing in Raleigh's demeanor was leering or suspicious. Inexplicably, she felt comfortable, as if she was right where she belonged.

"This is it." He unlocked a heavy door at the end of the hallway and let her step into the room first. He stepped in behind her, keeping the door open.

The room was larger than she expected, but she wasn't surprised to find it dark and lined with books from top to bottom on all four walls. Overstuffed chairs sat across from each other in front of a table, inviting one to read.

"No wonder you wanted to loan me a volume," she noted. "If you add even one more slim book to your collection, where will you find room for it?"

His pleasant laugh filled the room. "I can always find room for another book, I assure you." Immediately he strode to a shelf and retrieved a volume. "Here it is. The book I promised."

"How did you manage to find it so quickly?"

"The Dewey Decimal Classification System. I have implemented it here with great success."

"I don't think I know that system."

"I can explain it to you, if you like." Without pausing, he launched into a detailed and enthusiastic explanation of the ten main categories, followed by how they were further divided into call numbers based on the metric system. Eleanor grasped little of what Raleigh told her, but she had the distinct feeling that she would find more opportunities to learn all about the brilliant Melvil Dewey.

Monroe's voice interrupted. "Miss Kerr, your carriage awaits."

"Oh! Where has the time gone? I'm so sorry. I must depart, Raleigh." She tapped the volume. "I do thank you for loaning me this book. I shall begin reading it tonight."

"I eagerly await your insights." His eyes sparkled. Eleanor wondered if he were simply happy to find a new student or if his interest was based on more.

five

Two weeks later, Eleanor stood in the small entryway of Aunt Daphne's house and thumbed through several letters and bills that had just arrived by post. She stopped when she saw a cream-colored envelope addressed in elaborate script. The return address was familiar.

She gasped. "The Aldens!"

Eleanor shut the front door and hurried down the hall, her boot heels clacking against the hardwood. Upon reaching the entrance to her aunt's small study, she peered inside. "Aunt Daphne!"

"My dear child," she answered from her seat at the desk. Cook was standing in front of Daphne, no doubt receiving instructions about the week's menu or asking for yet another raise in the food budget. "Why are you in such a hurry? I could hear you running down the hall practically from the front door."

"I'm sorry." Eleanor held up the invitation. "But look! There is an invitation addressed to us."

Aunt Daphne chuckled. "Yes, we do receive invitations upon occasion. It's not as though I know no one in town. Most likely it is for the Strang wedding. I'll reply later."

Eleanor shook her head. "No. It's from the Aldens."

"The Aldens?"

"The Aldens?" The whites of Cook's eyes grew wide against her broad face. "Ain't they some fancy people you sew for, Miss Daphne?"

"Yes, they are an important family," Aunt Daphne agreed.

Eleanor nearly jumped up and down with excitement.

58

"Might we open it now?"

"Dear, dear. You are like a small child in your anticipation." Aunt Daphne's smile gave away her bemusement. "Since you're so eager to see what it is, why don't you open it?"

Eleanor picked up a letter opener from Aunt Daphne's desk and slit open the envelope at the fold. She drew out the invitation. "They're asking us to come to the dinner party."

Aunt Daphne nearly dropped her fountain pen. "The dinner party? The one we've been making dresses for all this time?"

"I know of no other."

Aunt Daphne's eyebrows arched as she set her pen down, but her expression didn't reveal the surprise that Eleanor had anticipated it would. "When I delivered her nightgown, Mrs. Alden mentioned something about including us, but I thought it was just idle talk. I never expected her to follow through."

"But she did!" Eleanor didn't bother to contain her zeal. "Oh, how wonderful of her to think of us! Or maybe it was Vera's idea. I do think she considers me rather a friend, you know."

Aunt Daphne contemplated Eleanor's statement. "Yes, I think she might. Still, I am a bit surprised."

Eleanor clutched the missive to her chest. "Might we accept?"

"Indeed, we must," her aunt answered. "I think not accepting would be unforgivable. Leave the invitation with me, and I will write a formal response as soon as I'm finished here."

Eleanor strode across the room and handed the invitation to her aunt. "Oh, thank you!"

Aunt Daphne wagged her finger at her niece. "But don't mention the invitation to them when you go over there today. That wouldn't be polite until I've had a chance to respond."

"Oh." She wasn't sure how she could conceal her excitement, but Eleanor understood her aunt. "Oh, but of course, I won't."

Eleanor practically danced out of the room. Imagine! She

would be going to the dinner party at the Aldens! She felt like Cinderella. Humming to herself, she made her way to the sewing room adjacent to the kitchen and gathered her supplies to make the trip to the Aldens'.

She wondered what type of dress she should wear. Aunt Daphne had a good number of the latest patterns in stock, so she would easily be able to find a fashionable style. Perhaps a dress with a sash to emphasize her tiny waist. She wondered if she should sew herself large sleeves or something closer to her arms. Which way should she go? She tapped her chin with her forefinger. Overblown sleeves were likely to make her look top-heavy, especially since she wasn't too tall. Something in the middle. Yes, that was the answer. Sleeves that weren't too large or too small, but just right. Like Goldilocks. She imagined the little fairy tale heroine eating three bowls of porridge and sitting in three chairs. Despite being many years older than the little girl in the story, Eleanor giggled.

What about the neckline? She knew many ladies seized the opportunity of an evening event to flaunt ample cleavage. Eleanor wondered what it would be like to enjoy the attention an immodest neckline would bring to her person. She quickly shook the thought out of her head. As a servant of Christ, she knew she had to suppress her vanity and remain reserved before a party of mixed company. The man she would one day marry would be sure to appreciate the fact that she valued herself enough to keep herself only for him. The thought sent a wave of heat to her cheeks. How could she—a maiden—let her mind wander to such imprudent thoughts!

She deliberately turned her mind to lace. Aunt Daphne had just received an order of lace from Ireland. Eleanor took in a breath when she recalled one particular pattern of delicate flowers crocheted with remarkable skill. Yes, she would add a bit of lace to the neckline, sleeves, and perhaps the hem. But the expense! She grimaced. Aunt Daphne would dock her pay to cover the cost, but to her mind, the sacrifice would be worth the result.

To ensure her aunt wouldn't promise the lace to someone else, Eleanor scurried into the sewing room to set it aside for herself. The box from Ireland still sat on the floor by the south wall—not a surprise since the sewing room remained in a perpetual state of organized chaos. Quickly she retrieved the intended lace from the box and was about to take it up to her room when several bolts of fabric caught her eye. Which one would she choose? She twisted her mouth. In order not to appear in the same fabric as someone else, she and her aunt would have to find out what other guests would be present and make sure to fashion their dresses out of something different. Eleanor's official time of mourning had finally passed, so she would be allowed to wear a color more daring than lavender. Yet the bright reds and yellows didn't speak to her. Her glance fell upon a bolt of rose-colored silk. Yes. That was it! Rose. Not too daring, but not too meek. Just right. She giggled once more.

The grandfather clock chimed the hour. She gasped when she remembered her appointment with Vera. She had to prepare to go to the Aldens'. Her thoughts taking a different turn, Eleanor hoped her new client would be pleased with her progress.

Smiling to herself, she folded the yellow gown with care so as not to wrinkle it too much. Vera was her favorite client out of the customers she had gained since arriving in Baltimore a few weeks ago. Some of the older matrons were fussy, and others wanted her to perform a magical feat with her sewing—as if her dresses would somehow take off decades and make them once again the center of attention. Still others bickered over the price even though they had chosen expensive fabrics, making Raleigh's protests seem mild in comparison. And some customers insisted on selecting styles that wouldn't flatter their figures, then blamed Eleanor when the dresses turned out exactly as she had predicted: unappealing. If she hadn't known better, she would have thought Aunt Daphne directed Eleanor to her most difficult clients, so she wouldn't need to please them anymore.

Her time in Baltimore had already proven trying, but she made sure not to complain to Papa. He had enough problems trying to reestablish himself in business back in New Orleans. Eleanor's gift to him was to give him no reason to worry about her.

In the letter she had written to Papa just that morning, Eleanor had focused on Vera. She was different from the rest of the ladies whom Eleanor had met. Shy, but not too shy to express an opinion, she seemed genuinely pleased with Eleanor's suggestions on color and style. Predictably, Vera looked beautiful in the frock Eleanor was in the process of fashioning for her—and she made sure to tell her so. Even Mrs. Alden's eyes lit with pleasure when she eyed her companion wearing the new dress. Surely Eleanor had pleased everyone who counted in the Alden house.

Eleanor sighed. She wished Vera could enjoy a life beyond that of being Mrs. Alden's companion. With her pleasing demeanor and gentle spirit, Vera could make a fine wife and mother. But when she hinted to Vera about her interests, Vera was reticent to say anything. She merely cast her gaze at the polished hardwood floors and let a shadow of a smile touch her lips. Eleanor fancied that Vera had some secret love. Maybe some mysterious man would come and sweep her off her feet one day. Eleanor hoped so.

"Maybe Vera's Mr. Right will be at the dinner party," she muttered to herself. "I remember they said something about Flint Jarvis. Hmm. I wonder about this Mr. Jarvis. Whoever could he be?"

She had little time to contemplate further since the hands on the clock were moving rapidly. Gathering her things,

Eleanor made a lively step into the hall and prepared herself to call out to her aunt that she was ready to depart. What a shock to discover Aunt Daphne waiting for her at the front door. Eleanor stopped in her tracks.

"I'll be going with you today to fit Vera's dress."

"Oh?" Eleanor knew disappointment showed in her voice. Over the past week, she had rather enjoyed going to the mansion alone, uninhibited by Aunt Daphne's watchful eye.

"Didn't I tell you?" Aunt Daphne asked as she slipped on her gloves. "I have an errand with the Aldens, too. In addition to the bedclothes she ordered from me, Mrs. Alden has decided to have a dress sewn for herself."

"A dress? So she'll be going to the dinner?"

"I don't think she would miss it for anything." Aunt Daphne looked out of the window on the side of the front door as if she were surveying the world itself and looking for Mrs. Alden on the horizon.

"I'm so glad to hear she wants to attend," Eleanor said. "It will do her good to get out of her bed for once."

"She very much enjoys the consideration that people give to the bedridden, I do believe," Aunt Daphne noted, returning her attention to Eleanor. "But the prospect of a party is even more pleasing. I'm glad her son is amenable to the idea. At first, I thought he might forbid it."

"Oh, he isn't as bad as all that." Eleanor twirled her white parasol, digging its end into the floor.

"You don't think so?" Aunt Daphne's tone of voice told Eleanor that her question was rhetorical. "I confess I'm a bit worried about your unbridled enthusiasm about this invitation from them. I don't want you getting grand ideas."

"I don't have any grand ideas." The parasol moved faster until Aunt Daphne shot her a warning look. Eleanor stopped twirling it abruptly.

"Oh? I understand from Mrs. Alden herself that you have

made a point of talking to Mr. Alden upon each visit."

Eleanor squirmed. Had Raleigh's mother been listening to every word they spoke while pretending indifference to their chatter? Or had Monroe tipped her off to their conversations? She performed a mental rundown of their exchanges and was grateful to realize she had never said a word to Raleigh that she believed to be contrary to her faith or social etiquette.

"I haven't made a point of talking to him," Eleanor said. "He's made a point of talking to me."

"Oh, is that the way it is? I wouldn't have pictured you as being quite so supercilious."

"Me?" Eleanor clutched her throat. She had never been described in such a way before, at least not to her face and not by one whose opinion mattered to her. "I don't mean to be so vain. It's just that. . .he always is present whenever I visit."

"And that pleases you?"

Eleanor didn't know how to respond. Ever since she had laid eyes on him and he had been so kind in light of her outburst and then even begun loaning her valuable books from his library, she had formed a fondness for him. So, of course, his presence delighted her, but she had the distinct feeling that her feelings weren't mirrored by Aunt Daphne. "The last time we conversed, he invited me to join the revival services at his church beginning next week. And I accepted."

"Without my leave?" Aunt Daphne sniffed and tugged at the waistline of her bright yellow dress.

"I didn't think I needed your leave to attend church. And of course," Eleanor added, making sure to soften her voice, "you are more than welcome to join us."

"I just might do that."

"You'd enjoy the services, I'm sure. Raleigh said the guest minister is quite energetic and gives a wondrous message whenever he preaches."

"Indubitably." Aunt Daphne's tone indicated she wasn't so

certain. She peered out of the window again.

"Raleigh has taken it upon himself to loan me some books from his library," Eleanor added. "Surely such attention is a privilege."

"Yes, he does seem to appreciate your intellect, which I admit, judging from our conversations on current affairs and the like, demonstrates your good schooling," Aunt Daphne conceded. "But are you sure that your mind is all he appreciates?"

"I hope he finds my appearance pleasing, although he has never mentioned anything." Eleanor self-consciously smoothed her beige skirt.

"I had hoped for a less ambiguous answer from you. I'm afraid you have disappointed me."

"Disappointed you? Why, I thought you would welcome any friendly overture from him since you yourself said he was quite difficult. Hasn't he been more pleasant since I started sewing for Vera?" Eleanor ventured, hoping the answer would be in the affirmative.

"Yes," her aunt conceded. "But in spite of the invitation we received, you must remember that you are only a seamstress. Any attentions from someone such as Raleigh Alden will only lead to trouble."

"Trouble?" Eleanor quivered.

Aunt Daphne glanced out the window once more before leaning closer to Eleanor. "Don't repeat this, but just last spring, one of the Blackston maids was sent away after she became too familiar with the elder son of the house."

Eleanor gasped. Mrs. Blackston was one of their best clients. She had just ordered two dresses for the fall season, and they expected her to place an order for at least two ball gowns for the winter holidays. "I don't believe it."

"She is a fine woman, and she did the best she could with her children. I don't fault her, even though her sons have quite the reputation."

"Of course, she is not to blame. A devout parent does not guarantee religious children," Eleanor said. "God has no grandchildren."

"True. Nevertheless, you don't want any part of such scandal."

"Aunt Daphne! You know me better than that!" Eleanor protested. "Besides, I think we are more than servants to the Aldens. Why, even though I've only known her a short time, I consider Vera a friend. And Raleigh certainly has an excellent reputation."

"True," Aunt Daphne admitted. "I just hope he lives up to it."

"He does. He has always been nothing but a consummate gentleman in my presence. I'm sure his interest in me is only intellectual and spiritual. That's all." She lifted her forefinger for emphasis.

"Indeed? And he cannot find someone in his own set to share conversation with? Someone like Miss Vera Howard, perhaps?"

"Vera?" The young woman had never confided or even hinted at any interest in Raleigh other than as her employer. "I would imagine he could converse with her anytime he pleases. And I'm sure he does."

"Unless he is talking with you, instead."

"Don't be silly, Aunt Daphne. I am not standing in anyone's way."

"I hope not." She gathered her supplies and lavender parasol, which matched the lavender accents on her dress. "In any event, I was so in hopes that you wouldn't set your cap for anyone at all, at least for a few years."

"Oh, I'm sure I can stay in business with you as long as you need me."

"Not only that, but we should take this opportunity to travel together. I've saved up a little money, and as soon as you gather a little nest egg, we can take a fine tour abroad.

Perhaps even sail on a steamship to worlds unknown to us."
Aunt Daphne stared ahead, her look vacant as though she
were concentrating on a picture in her mind instead of the
copper-colored walls.

Eleanor tried not to cringe. This wasn't the first time her aunt
had broached the subject of world travel. Over time, she had
developed the distinct feeling that her aunt only agreed to her
extended presence in her home so she could cultivate another
woman to share her dream of travel. But alas, even with all the
hints and talk, Eleanor still had not developed the desire to see
the world. The most adventure she craved was reading about
Old Testament battles. How could she tell her aunt she had
chosen the wrong person to be a traveling companion?

Eleanor sent up a silent prayer when the carriage pulled
up, meaning she didn't have to decide to reveal her feelings at
present.

"Finally! I thought Henry would never get here. Let us be
on our way." Without further ado, Aunt Daphne strode out
the door, and Eleanor followed her.

The ride to the Aldens' was silent except for the *clip-
clop* of the horses' hooves and the sounds of the city streets
teeming with people, horses, carriages, carts, and streetcars.
Eleanor thought about Aunt Daphne's admonitions. Surely
Raleigh didn't have his eye on Vera. But if he did, how could
she interfere? Indeed, how could she be so bold as to think
she would have the power to stand between them, even if
she tried? She shook her head, tossing the very thought out
of her mind.

Perhaps her fears would be allayed once she saw Raleigh
that day. After all, wasn't he the one who was responsible for
her being invited to the dinner? Surely he was. Who else?

But despite Eleanor's hopes, she was disappointed to find
that Raleigh didn't greet her as usual. Perhaps he didn't realize
she had an appointment at that hour. Then again, she hadn't

finished with the latest book she had borrowed, so Raleigh had no reason to greet her. Perhaps she had told Aunt Daphne more of the truth than she originally hoped. Perhaps Raleigh's interest in her really was only spiritual and intellectual.

Moments later, Eleanor set only half her mind to the appointment as she watched Mrs. Alden inspect Aunt Daphne's work.

"Yes, I do believe this color is quite appropriate for me. I do so like mint green. So fresh and lively for late summer," Mrs. Alden said.

"It will bring out the green in your eyes."

"As if anyone will be paying any attention to my old eyes." Mrs. Alden let out a laugh.

"Oh, I'm sure you will be the belle of the ball," Aunt Daphne said.

"No, I imagine one of our young girls will be," Mrs. Alden said.

"I quite imagine that Vera will be the belle of the ball," Eleanor speculated.

"Oh, pshaw. You are too kind," Vera said.

Eleanor studied her client. Her blush indicated that despite her protests, she hoped something would develop. Eleanor prayed it would.

"I do hope you're planning to accept our invitation to the dinner," Mrs. Alden said. "I trust it arrived."

"Yes, ma'am," Aunt Daphne answered. "And, of course, I do plan to respond in the affirmative. We are so pleased to be included."

"Included in what?" a male voice interrupted.

Eleanor instantly recognized the tenor. Her heart betrayed her with a lurch. Before turning in the direction of the voice, she made sure to set her expression in a neutral fashion so as not to make obvious her feelings. As usual, Vera shyly cast her eyes downward. Aunt Daphne's face adopted an icy refrain.

"Raleigh!" Mrs. Alden addressed her son. "Don't you believe in knocking first?"

"I would have, but as you can see, my hands are occupied." He hovered in the doorway and tilted his head toward the tray of tea and biscuits he held. "Besides, I surmised that if you ladies weren't decent, the door would have been shut."

"Where is Monroe?" Mrs. Alden asked.

"I was on my way upstairs, so I offered to bring tea myself. I hope you ladies don't mind." He nodded to each one as he entered and set the tray down on the proper table. "Besides, if I don't offer to take on Monroe's duties now and again, I lose out on all the gossip. You ladies were saying?" His eyes twinkled, reminding Eleanor of how Saint Nicholas looked in pictures so popular around Christmastide.

Mrs. Alden didn't seem to mind answering. "I was just saying to Daphne and Eleanor that I do hope they'll accept my invitation to the dinner."

"Oh?" Raleigh's dark eyebrows arched, then he smiled as if forcing himself. "My, but we have expanded our guest list greatly, have we not?"

Eleanor hoped she managed to hide her upset. So he was shocked that they were included? And after she had all but insisted that he had been the one who was responsible for their inclusion. Why did he act as though he didn't want them there at all? She felt tears threaten.

Heavenly Father, help me! Have I really developed such strong feelings already? What is wrong with me? What was I thinking?

"This dinner party isn't for the society pages. We can always put on a ball for them later. I just want everyone who means anything to our family to be there," Mrs. Alden proclaimed. "A small affair, really."

"But, of course, I would be delighted for both Miss Kerrs to be present." He smiled at each of them. "I do hope you will be in attendance."

"But, of course," Aunt Daphne assured.

Eleanor contented herself with a slight nod. So Raleigh Alden wanted them there as long as the event wasn't meant for the society pages. As long as he could keep them under wraps, he could pretend not to know them but as seamstresses. As much as she hated to admit it, maybe her aunt was right. Maybe Raleigh Alden was nothing but a snob.

She thought about her earlier silliness when she had run into Aunt Daphne's room and found the Irish lace. She wished she hadn't bothered. One of her old dresses would have to do.

No, even better, she didn't have to go to the party at all.

six

"Aunt Daphne, I feel a bit puny." Eleanor leaned against the doorframe of her aunt's bedroom. She clutched her stomach and groaned.

"You've been feeling a bit puny for a while now." Aunt Daphne placed the palm of her hand on Eleanor's forehead. "You don't seem feverish."

"No. I'll be all right."

"First you bowed out of going to the revival and now this." She crossed her arms in obvious displeasure. "Don't tell me you don't want to see Raleigh."

Eleanor swallowed. How had her aunt learned so much about her in such a short time?

Aunt Daphne adjusted the sleeve on her emerald green evening dress, which looked well against the light green paint and white cotton curtains decorating her generous room, then turned from her vanity mirror to inspect her niece. Her mouth straightened itself into a tight line. "Don't be ridiculous, child. Raleigh Alden is just a man. And you'll be meeting many more at the party."

"I don't want to meet more men. And my stomach really does hurt." She spoke the truth. Eleanor's stomach pained her and had been protesting off and on for several days, regardless of how much or how little she ate. Even restricting herself to chicken soup hadn't helped. Eleanor entered the room and reclined on the bed, a large affair covered with a blanket crocheted from cream-colored tobacco twine.

"You finished your dress, didn't you?"

"Yes, ma'am."

She had deliberately dawdled over sewing her own dress. But even though she had tried to beg off with the excuse that she was too swamped with orders from clients, Aunt Daphne wouldn't budge. Once she saw Eleanor's outdated gowns, she insisted that Eleanor make herself a new one. "I sewed the last bit of lace on the sleeves this morning."

"Good." She shot Eleanor a look through narrowed eyelids. "Judging by the looks of things, you won't get into your dress in time to go. But that's your plan, isn't it?"

Eleanor swallowed before setting the dress on her lap. "I don't understand, Aunt Daphne. Why the sudden change of heart? I thought you didn't want me to go to the dinner. Now you seem as though you want nothing more."

Aunt Daphne cleared her throat. "I just didn't want you getting grand ideas, that's all. I can only be thankful that my best client saw fit to include us in her plans. Of course, we cannot insult her by sending regrets at the last moment."

"I suppose not." Still, Eleanor had the feeling that her aunt wasn't being totally honest.

"Now look here, child," Aunt Daphne remonstrated. "We accepted the invitation, and we're going to go whether we want to or not. I want you to go to your room and get dressed now. And do something with that hair. I'll call Ginny to help you."

Seeing that even sickness wouldn't excuse her from their social obligation, Eleanor sat up, then rose to her feet. "That's all right. I can dress myself."

"What about the buttons in the back?"

Eleanor had forgotten about those. In an effort to add interest to her gown, she had sewn a row of silk-covered buttons a half inch apart from the tip of the neck to the point of the waist. Even with a buttonhook, Ginny would most likely struggle to secure her in the dress.

Aunt Daphne seemed to read her mind. "Yes, vanity is expensive, isn't it?"

Eleanor remembered the cost of the Irish lace. "Yes, it is. Expensive, indeed."

"You'd best get going. The carriage is due to arrive in less than an hour," her aunt advised. "Did Ginny bring you the soup and bread as I asked?"

"Yes, but I'm not hungry. Besides, we'll be eating dinner at the Aldens'. At least, that's what I thought."

"Of course, we'll be eating dinner at the Aldens'. But you certainly don't want to go there on an empty stomach. You'll be too hungry."

"I don't understand."

Aunt Daphne clucked her tongue. "Poor girl. Your mother wasn't able to teach you, was she? And of course, your father wouldn't be expected to teach you proper etiquette regarding a dinner party. Men aren't supposed to know our little secrets."

"Secrets?"

"Yes. Always go to a dinner party—or any other type of social event—on a full stomach. Then you will be able to resist the urge to overeat while you're there."

"You think I overeat?" Eleanor inspected her waist, which didn't show any evidence of a large appetite.

"Of course not. But you don't want to eat as you normally would, because if you do, you may appear to be unladylike. Men watch for those signs."

Eleanor thought back to her earlier years when she enjoyed the camaraderie of social gatherings and partook of delicious food without worrying about criticism. "Aunt Daphne, I don't intend any disrespect, but isn't what you suggest just a bit deceptive?"

"Many a happy marriage is based upon a little bit of deception."

Eleanor wasn't sure how her aunt's cynical statement could be accurate. And since Aunt Daphne had never married, Eleanor questioned her wisdom. Still, she decided to keep her thoughts to herself. "I suppose I'd better be getting dressed."

"Good. Meet me at the front door when you're ready."

&

An hour and a half later, the carriage pulled in front of the Aldens' home, and the driver assisted the ladies in disembarking. No other carriages were positioned in the driveway.

"Apparently we are the last guests to arrive," Aunt Daphne noted.

"I'm certain we're not so very late," Eleanor said in spite of the fact that she wasn't so sure. She could only hope that her declaration would spare her a speech from her aunt on her tardiness in preparing for the party.

Aunt Daphne contented herself by glancing at her with steely eyes, using her sharp peripheral vision. Eleanor concluded that the coach driver's presence prompted her aunt's effort to refrain from dispensing a lecture.

Eleanor had followed her aunt's advice and eaten a half bowl of Cook's delicious soup and the hot roll provided. As much as she longed for the freedom of childhood that allowed one to eat as one pleased, perhaps her aunt was right. At least her stomach wouldn't embarrass her by growling before dinner, although pains reminded her of its presence now and again.

Monroe answered the front door and directed them to the parlor. The floor and furniture had been waxed to a high gloss for the occasion. Not a knickknack was turned in an odd direction. The candlesticks were filled with new beeswax tapers at least a foot in height.

Instantly, Eleanor felt Raleigh's gaze upon her. She sensed that he had been anticipating her arrival. When she sent him a shy look, interest lit his eyes. Then she remembered his surprise that she and her aunt had been invited to this event. Perhaps he merely noticed her because she was his guest?

He strode over to them and exchanged a brief greeting with

her aunt before turning toward her. "Good evening, Eleanor."

"Good evening." Knowing that to do less would be impolite, she extended her hand in greeting. Not hesitating to take the opportunity, he surprised her by brushing his lips briefly against the back of her hand above the knuckles. She became conscious of her rapidly beating heart.

"I trust by your presence here that you are feeling well?"

"Yes, better, thank you." Indeed, her stomach pains had subsided, though they had been replaced by regret that she hadn't gone to the revival with Raleigh. Perhaps her stomach's protests had been spurred by anxiety rather than by a physical malady.

"If I may say so, you look exceptionally lovely tonight."

His words made her every doubt disintegrate. "I am quite pleased that you do say so. And your observation has made me feel more beautiful than I have since. . .since. . ."

Before my mother died.

She couldn't express herself. Instead, her gaze landed on the floor, where she got a good look at Raleigh's black leather wing-tipped shoes.

"I'm as tongue-tied as a schoolgirl. I must look like such a ninny," she murmured.

"Not at all," Raleigh answered.

Although she hadn't intended on his hearing her, Raleigh's response gave her the courage to look into his face.

"I know you have just come out of mourning," he added. "Don't worry. Before you know it, you'll feel at ease at a little soiree such as this—just as if you were drinking tea in your own parlor."

She looked about the room, where the small number of partygoers dressed in finery mingled. "I don't know."

"How about if we find out?" He extended his elbow so she could take his arm. "If I may?" He looked at Eleanor, then Aunt Daphne.

"I hope you don't plan to monopolize her all evening," Aunt Daphne warned. "After all, this is her first time out since my dear sister-in-law passed on."

"Aunt Daphne!" Eleanor admonished. How could her aunt say such a bold thing to their host?

"I'll try not to impose too much," he assured her with a chuckle. "I never force my attentions upon any lady."

"Indeed." Aunt Daphne sent him a sly smile and, with a wave of her fan, strode to another part of the room.

"And you would never need to do so," Eleanor hastened to assure him. "I'm so glad you greeted us in any event. I need to return the book I borrowed." She handed him the small volume that she had been holding since her arrival.

"Already? My, but you are a fast reader." He set the book on a nearby occasional table next to a small mixed bouquet of summer wildflowers in a cut crystal vase.

"Indeed? I thought myself rather a slow one. I've been sewing many dresses and gowns as of late and have had very little time to delve into reading aside from my morning and evening devotions."

Mrs. Alden's voice rang through the room. "Raleigh!"

Raleigh looked over at the corner where his mother sat, with Aunt Daphne hovering by her hostess seated in a blue velvet and mahogany chair. She crooked her finger, motioning for him to join her. Raleigh nodded and moved his elbow forward. "Why don't we start with my mother?"

"Are you sure?"

"Of course, I'm sure. You don't think you'll get away with not speaking to your hostess, do you?" His tone was teasing.

"And I have no desire to avoid her. She has always been delightful to me." She sent him a smile and followed him to his mother's perch.

Mrs. Alden was, as expected, dressed in the mint green dress that Aunt Daphne had sewn for her. Elaborate embellishments had taken Aunt Daphne a week of almost constant work to sew, but the effort had been worthwhile as far as demonstrating her aunt's sewing expertise. Had Mrs. Alden been her client, Eleanor would have advised her to appear in a dress with fewer adornments, so she could look more dignified as would have been appropriate for a woman of advancing years. But Aunt Daphne had said she didn't care if Mrs. Alden wanted to dress like a schoolgirl—her job was to make her happy. Funny, she didn't look too happy at the moment.

"Raleigh," Mrs. Alden said as soon as proper greetings were exchanged, "have you seen to it that Eleanor is introduced to Mr. Jarvis?"

"She only just arrived." Oddly, Raleigh seemed to be trying to hold back an irritation that had been missing earlier. "Of course, I'll introduce them, Mother. I had no indication there was any special hurry."

Mrs. Alden cleared her throat. "I want all of our guests to become acquainted, of course."

Eleanor surveyed the room. Vera was standing by the fireplace. Unable to control her emotions, she swallowed with pride when she noticed how well Vera's dress looked on her. They had worked together to choose a flattering style and pleasing embellishments, and the result appeared to be a great success. For a moment, Eleanor wished more people were present to appreciate her handiwork. Gaining new admirers would only increase her sewing business.

A proverb from scripture popped into her head. "He that is greedy of gain troubleth his own house."

She sighed. "Yes, Lord, I know I have enough."

"What was that?" Raleigh asked.

She flinched. "Oh, nothing. I'm sorry. I was just admiring. . . uh. . .everything."

"Why, thank you, Eleanor." Mrs. Alden's smile looked self-congratulatory. "Now run along, Raleigh, and introduce

Eleanor to our other guests."

Eleanor realized that Mrs. Alden didn't mention any need for Aunt Daphne to meet the guests. She looked to her aunt. "Don't you want to meet everyone else, too?"

"Oh, I'll have plenty of time to talk to everyone. You know me. I'm a regular social butterfly. You two go right ahead."

Eleanor nodded, hoping the gesture disguised her wonder. Her aunt didn't seem to be the least bit vexed by what Eleanor would have perceived as a slight. Furthermore, she had cautioned Raleigh not to keep her all evening, yet she had moments later encouraged her to stay by Raleigh's side to be introduced to the other guests. Sometimes Eleanor just couldn't discern what her aunt was thinking.

She glanced at Raleigh. He had pursed his lips. Perhaps he didn't like being told to run along. Eleanor suppressed a chuckle as he led her to where Vera conversed with a man whom Eleanor could only assume was the fabled Flint Jarvis. Dressed in fine style, he appeared in a black evening suit that flattered a trim physique. Eleanor didn't find his aquiline nose or slightly protruding lips appealing, but when he laughed, apparently at some witty comment that Eleanor couldn't hear, his countenance seemed pleasant enough. Eleanor sent a conspiratorial smile Vera's way. Apparently when she was with an attractive man, Vera could display formidable wit and charm.

Eleanor eyed two other men not far away who seemed to be engaged in their own conversation. The first was short and stocky, and while his appearance wasn't displeasing, she saw nothing memorable about him. The second seemed close to Mrs. Alden's age. His black hair was streaked with gray, but his eyes were lively. Eleanor guessed the two had been invited to round out her dinner table. No doubt since invitations from the Aldens were desirable and they were known for employing the best cook in town, the bachelors were more than happy to oblige.

Dinner. Now there was a thought. Pleasant odors wafted in from the back of the house. Surely the bell to summon them would be ringing soon. Funny, her stomach no longer ailed her at all. Why did being near Raleigh make her feel so much better? Now that she was close to him, she realized that she didn't mind the fact she was being led toward a strange man she had never met.

Raleigh made the introductions with practiced skill.

Flint Jarvis gave Eleanor a passing glance but didn't seem to register much fascination with her. Instead, he spoke to Raleigh. "Have I seen you since I returned from my trip to the Orient?"

"No, I don't believe we have conversed since I moved back to Baltimore."

"The Orient?" Eleanor couldn't help but note. "A journey there sounds quite exotic—and dangerous, Mr. Jarvis."

"Oh, please. *Mr. Jarvis* is my father. Do call me Flint."

Eleanor cut her glance to Raleigh, who sent her a small nod. She wasn't sure why she sought his approval. Still, she was glad he didn't seem to think she would be too bold by accepting Flint's invitation to call him by his Christian name.

"Speaking of names," Raleigh said, smiling at Eleanor. "Flint prides himself on his middle name."

"Oh, what is that?"

"Danger, my girl," Flint answered.

"Danger? Your mother named you *Danger?*"

As the two men burst into laughter, she soon realized why her remark seemed so amusing to them. Flint had been speaking metaphorically, but she had jumped to the conclusion that he had been speaking in the literal sense. Eleanor felt a warm blush rise to her cheeks. *They both must think me a ninny!*

"Oh, I see the joke now," she managed.

"I did catch you off guard, which is understandable," Raleigh said. "I beg your forgiveness."

"None needed," she responded. "I may be the source of amusement one moment, but the joke will be on someone else next time."

"How admirable," Raleigh said.

"I agree," Flint noted. "My real middle name is not that imaginative, though I never run away from a challenge. I know all there is to know about my friend Raleigh, so Miss Kerr, why don't you tell me about your travels?"

"My travels?" Eleanor squirmed. "I'm afraid there is not much to tell."

"Oh? It was my understanding that you aren't from around here."

"Oh, I'm not. But my train trip from Louisiana to Baltimore is the extent of my adventures. And I'm afraid I didn't enjoy the journey enough to be eager to travel more in the future."

"Then maybe you should have taken a luxury train car."

"Perhaps that would have helped." As soon as she realized her confession was an admission that she couldn't afford such expensive train accommodations, again a flush of embarrassment filled her. Truly she was among a class of people where she was out of place.

"Eleanor is a fine businesswoman," Raleigh said. "She is wise not to waste her money on frivolities that only offer temporary pleasure."

Eleanor sent him a grateful look.

"Like the dresses the ladies are wearing tonight?" Flint joked. "I should say a pretty penny was spent on them all."

"And rightfully so," Raleigh hastened to defend her. "Besides, I'm sure they can wear their dresses to many events."

Flint raised his eyebrows. "Then you don't know women, my boy."

"Excuse me," Eleanor said. "It's been lovely meeting you, but I must speak to my aunt."

"I surely hope we will be seated near one another this evening," Flint said. "I would enjoy hearing about your aspirations of seeing the world. Surely you have some despite your protests to the contrary."

"No, indeed. I'm afraid I have no aspirations to see the world. Even if I could travel in luxury, I don't think I would take the opportunity. Reading about Old Testament battles is adventure enough for me."

"Well, that is disappointing to hear."

"I'm sorry," she apologized even though she didn't know why she should have to express regret over her basic personality. She was the way God made her, and she knew He had made no mistake. Then she remembered someone else God made—someone who was more like the type of woman Flint sought. "My aunt wishes to travel. Isn't that right, Raleigh?"

He paused, then nodded quickly. "We've never discussed it, but Eleanor certainly knows her aunt better than I. Together they operate a business sewing fine and frivolous dresses for the local ladies."

"Oh." Flint's eyes took on a glint of embarrassment. Eleanor guessed he wouldn't have made such disparaging comments about the ladies' dresses had he known. "Oh, indeed. And a fine business I'm sure it is. Anyone who helps our local ladies to appear happier and more beautiful is only doing our fine city proud."

"Thank you."

"So." He looked around the room. "Am I to assume your aunt is the redhead talking to Mrs. Alden?"

"Yes, she is."

Flint put his hands on his hips and inspected Aunt Daphne. Eleanor wasn't sure she felt so comfortable with how he seemed to take in every detail of her appearance. Seeming to notice she was being observed, Aunt Daphne shot her gaze toward him. To Eleanor's shock, she could almost see bolts of lightning flash back and forth between their eyes.

Raleigh appeared to sense the immediate attraction, as well. "I'm assuming you won't object, Flint, if I introduce you properly."

"Not at all." Flint's voice didn't hide his eagerness.

"If you will pardon me," Eleanor said, "I should like to speak to Vera."

The men nodded, and she was excused.

As Eleanor stepped over to her friend and client, who had just broken away from a conversation, she thought about Raleigh. He had not been the least bit miffed at her for bowing out of going to revival services at his church and had defended her to the limit when Flint made tactless remarks. How could she stay upset with him? She couldn't.

Reaching Vera, Eleanor touched her shoulder. "Vera! You look gorgeous."

"Thank you. You did a fine job on my dress." Vera's lips barely moved as she spoke. While she was never one to be overly expressive and ebullient, her manner seemed stilted, even for one so prim.

"Thank you, but it's not just the dress," Eleanor assured her, touching her sleeve. "Your beauty always shines."

"You do exaggerate."

"Not in the least."

Vera didn't seem eager to continue their conversation. Surely she wasn't suddenly taking on an air of snobbery simply because they were among a few of the Aldens' intimates. Eleanor decided to wait and see what Vera would do next.

Vera looked around the room as though searching for another person to approach. Her gaze rested a little longer on Raleigh than it should have. Eleanor considered commenting on how dashing their host appeared on this particular evening but thought better of it.

"Are you having a good time?" Vera asked, apparently

deciding that escape from Eleanor was impossible at the moment.

A sense of sadness filled Eleanor at the thought. Perhaps she had misjudged the extent of Vera's warm feelings toward her, after all. In the meantime, Eleanor wasn't sure how best to respond to Vera's query.

Grateful even to be included in the evening, she searched for a truthful statement. "I haven't been out in so long. This is truly a blessing for me. I'm so appreciative of being included." As soon as she made mention of the last sentiment, Eleanor regretted how much she sounded like the grateful servant rather than a woman who could hold her own amid the other guests. She could only conclude that Flint and his thoughtless comments had unnerved her more than she realized.

"I see you've met Flint Jarvis," Vera noted, looking over toward the bachelors as they conversed with Eleanor's aunt. "Isn't he debonair?"

"Uh, yes. Yes, he is. He seems to have many excellent stories about his travels."

Vera sighed. "I haven't had the privilege of speaking to him at length, but he did share an anecdote with me earlier this evening." Her glance roved toward Flint, and she let out another sigh.

Eleanor let out a little gasp. "Vera! I do believe you're becoming smitten!"

Vera stared at her hands, clasped at her waist, as though they had become an extreme source of interest.

Eleanor placed her hand on Vera's. "Oh, you must take every chance you can to converse with him."

Fear lit Vera's eyes. "No. Never!"

"Never? But why not?"

Vera shook her head. "Never. That's all I have to say."

seven

•

Vera and Eleanor had moved to a group of chairs off to the side, hoping to mute the noise from some of the louder party-goers. Raleigh chose to break away from his conversation across the room and join them. Nevertheless, Eleanor was determined to get to the bottom of Vera's strange behavior. At the same time, she didn't want to embarrass the young woman in front of Raleigh or make an issue out of the fact that Vera seemed especially interested in a conversation her aunt and Flint Jarvis were having near the punch table.

She kept her voice low. "Vera, why wouldn't you want to speak to Mr. Jarvis? This is a party, after all. Aren't you sup-posed to converse with all the guests?" Eleanor knew her friend was shy, but she hadn't expected her to react so vio-lently at the idea of talking to a man. "And certainly he would be flattered by your attentions."

Vera crossed her arms and stared at Flint, who was holding court by the unlit gray stone fireplace as he spoke to enrap-tured guests. "I won't debate that point. Isn't any man flat-tered by the attentions of any woman?"

"Vera!" Raleigh intervened. "Do you really hold us men in such low esteem?"

"Aren't you flattered by the attentions of all women?" Her lips tightened as her chin tilted upward.

"Only the pretty ones." The mischievous look in his eyes showed that he spoke in jest. Yet when he offered a glimpse to Eleanor, she knew he meant to say she was one of the pretty ones.

Eleanor fanned herself in the vain hope that she might

discourage a blush. "I'm sure he'd be delighted to have you listen to his accounts of travel to the Orient. I'm afraid I was quite a disappointment to him as an audience."

"You? I can't imagine that you would be a disappointment to anyone," Vera's voice was devoid of sarcasm.

"Hear, hear," Raleigh agreed.

Eleanor's feelings toward Raleigh were growing more tender by the moment. "I appreciate your vote of confidence, however misplaced it may be. Aunt Daphne wants me to be a traveling companion for her, but alas, I have no interest in world travel."

"I see no fault in that," Raleigh assured her.

"Neither do I," Vera agreed, "but I do believe it would be quite glamorous to take a steamship cruise."

"In first class, of course. I fancy that steerage isn't quite what you have in mind," Raleigh noted.

"I can't even afford steerage." As though she suddenly realized the implication of what she said, Vera turned an apologetic face to Raleigh. "Not that you aren't quite generous to me, Raleigh. I sometimes feel as though I hardly do enough to earn my keep."

"I assure you, though I love my mother dearly, I have no doubt that you earn more than your keep. I would be at a loss to keep her in the good humor that she stays in because of your devoted companionship to her."

"Thank you."

"If only she were in robust health, then I could contemplate the possibility of sending you both off on a cruise together." He folded his arms and peered at the corner of the ceiling. Eleanor could almost see the cogs turning in his head. "Perhaps with her doctor's permission. . ."

"Again, I thank you, but that is quite all right. I'm not sure such a situation is what I had in mind." Vera's posture slumped, a sign Eleanor took as a gesture of defeat. She wondered why Vera acted so.

Eleanor decided to change the subject. "I must say, Mr. Jarvis seems to have a lot of leisure time to make complicated journeys. I wonder what his business is." She took a sudden interest in a bouquet of summer flowers atop an occasional table, so she could avoid eye contact with either Raleigh or Vera. Asking about a person's source of income bordered on discourtesy, but she had to wonder.

"I don't know all the details, but he has told me he keeps an office near the harbor," Raleigh told her.

Eleanor nodded, even though she still wasn't sure what he meant. Did Mr. Jarvis hold an ordinary job? If so, he would never have the time or the financial resources to enjoy such an extravagant lifestyle. But if he was an heir or was independently wealthy through some other means, why would he need an office near the wharf? She wanted to ask more but knew that to probe would be the height of rudeness. She had been bold enough to show any interest in his employment.

She watched as Vera looked over at Flint and his rapt audience. "Mr. Jarvis doesn't seem the least bit disappointed in your aunt."

Eleanor inspected the twosome. "Indeed." She raised her eyebrows despite her best attempts not to appear shocked. She had never seen her aunt look so ebullient and alive. Considering her proclivity for attention-getting bright colors and her lack of reticence in any situation, that feat was quite an accomplishment.

"Yes, I'd say the two of them don't need me. They seem to be getting along splendidly," Raleigh said. "Why, they are so engrossed in their own conversation that I don't believe they even noticed earlier when I excused myself."

Eleanor held back an expression of surprise. Who would have thought that her aunt would become so animated with the evening's mystery man? Setting the puzzlement out of her mind, she decided to address Raleigh. "I can't imagine anyone being so obtuse as not to notice your absence."

"So you would miss me should I go away?" An expectant light haunted his eyes.

Surprised by his response, Eleanor realized that her statement had been too bold. She searched for the proper quip. "Oh, you are such a jokester." She resisted the urge to touch his arm, choosing instead to fan herself.

"Do you really think I am joking?"

Vera rescued her. "Raleigh, really, must you be so probing?"

Eleanor sent her an appreciative look. To her surprise, she caught something strange in Vera's expression—almost as though she were peeved. But over what? Surely Raleigh's silly question hadn't provoked her so.

"I beg pardon," Raleigh apologized. "I suppose I'm caught up in the romance of the evening." He looked at Eleanor but not long enough for her to return his gaze.

"It's so lovely to watch two people become enamored with one another." Vera's voice held a hint of wistfulness. "Don't you agree, Raleigh?"

"Indeed." Raleigh looked into Eleanor's eyes.

His repeated gestures sent her stomach into a pleasant lurch. She wanted to look into his eyes in a daring way but discovered she couldn't overcome her sudden feeling of shyness.

"Indeed," Vera said.

Eleanor turned her attention to her friend. Vera's voice seemed clipped, almost as though she were vexed. Why would Vera have any reason to be vexed? Unless she was jealous of Aunt Daphne. Yes, she reasoned. She was jealous of Aunt Daphne. That had to be the reason for her sudden foul mood.

"Vera," Eleanor said, "why don't you join Aunt Daphne and Mr. Jarvis?"

"Me?" Vera cut her gaze to the pair. "But they look as though they are conversing quite well without any distraction."

"Oh, I'm sure they won't mind."

"But your aunt, Daphne. . ."

"Don't vex yourself about her."

"But Mr. Jarvis seems so enamored with her," Vera objected.

"Perhaps, but she has no intention of following up on any prospective suitors. Marriage is the farthest thing from her mind," Eleanor assured her, and she meant it.

"Eleanor's right," Raleigh agreed. "Are you not aware that— if you'll pardon me—but isn't Miss Kerr at least ten years older than Mr. Jarvis?" He looked to Eleanor with a searching expression.

"Far be it from me to tell her age."

Raleigh chuckled. "Of course. What was I thinking? But to look at them, well, let's just say that an odd match they would make, certainly."

"Certainly," Eleanor didn't hesitate to concur.

"So Vera, do go on and join them," Raleigh encouraged her.

"Well, all right." Vera excused herself and headed toward the gregarious twosome.

Eleanor watched her aunt's expression go from enchanted to irked. A guilty pang shot through her. Had she been wrong to let Raleigh encourage Vera?

"Now, my dear," Raleigh said, "will you not join me in a fresh glass of lemonade?"

My dear? Had he just called her *my dear*? A shiver of happiness traveled up and down her spine. "Oh, yes. But of course."

ꙮ

Later over dinner, Raleigh watched as Flint kept his attentions directed at Daphne. Poor Vera tried her mightiest to attract his interest, but no matter how often she attempted to divert attention to herself, Flint found some way to turn the conversation back to the elder seamstress.

Raleigh wouldn't have believed the turn of events if he

hadn't been there to witness them himself. He felt pity for Vera. The girl was shy and easily blended in with the beige wallpaper patterned with blue roses in their dining room. He wished Vera and Eleanor had remembered the hue of paper before dressing Vera. He suppressed a sigh as he watched her do her best to put on a show of confidence, batting her long lashes at Flint, touching her coiffure with her fingertips to attract attention to her hair and face, talking just a notch too loudly. He had never seen the girl act in such a manner.

Eleanor, on the other hand, was her usual composed self. No matter what the circumstance, she always seemed to know what to say, the proper inflection of voice to employ, and when to comment. Though she was a mere seamstress, Eleanor conducted herself with the poise of a woman trained for much larger expectations in life. He had a feeling that moving to Baltimore had been a comedown for her.

He had concluded that seeming out of place was a factor that attracted them to each another. Beginning a new life in a different location was never easy, as he had learned from his recent relocation. Everyone—even people one may have known before—was but a stranger. He could only hope that this little dinner made Eleanor feel just a bit less alone.

Not that she would be alone for long. Her smooth skin was touched by pink in her cheeks. Stunning eyes glimmered in the candlelight. Why hadn't he taken closer notice before? He suppressed a sigh. She was the image of modern loveliness, reminding him of a ladies' periodical advertisement for the latest beauty cream. Surely Flint would have been attentive to her the entire evening had she not rebuffed his only interest—traveling the world.

Flint. What an unlikely match for Eleanor, in any event. At least he thought as much. He eyed his mother, who beamed as she relished her long-forgotten role as belle of the ball. Years had melted from her face. If he hadn't known better, he would have thought that she fancied herself a teenager again, hold-ing court among all her guests, including a number of pro-spective suitors. Yet her eyes kept darting back and forth from Flint, to Eleanor, then back again. Why did he sense that this evening's mission was more than just to reunite friends and acquaintances to celebrate his return? Could matchmaking have been a secret agenda? And if so, for whom?

He couldn't help but wonder. If Mother had hoped that Vera would find a suitor, judging from the girl's interest in Flint, she could count the evening a success. Yet he couldn't imagine that Mother would want her companion, a young woman of whom she thought highly, to marry and hence leave her employment. Then why? What intrigue was hap-pening before his eyes that he was witnessing but could not decipher?

Not wishing Vera to make a fool of herself, Raleigh resolved to engage her in conversation from time to time, hoping to lure her away from her obvious grabs at Flint's attention. He wondered what topic of conversation might interest his mother's companion.

"So, Vera," he ventured, "how do you think Mother's new liniment is working for her?"

"She seems to be doing better with it, thank you." Question answered, Vera smiled, then turned her face back toward Flint, who was outlining his plans to explore the Caribbean.

As soon as was polite, Raleigh tried again. "Vera, what book are you reading now?"

When she turned back toward him this time, the look on her face conveyed no interest or pleasure. "Dickens."

He waited for her to name the Charles Dickens title, but she didn't comply. "A fine author, indeed." He opened his mouth to elaborate, but she cut him off.

"Yes. Quite intriguing." With that, she lifted her spoon to partake of the lobster bisque and tilted her head toward Flint, who still held his audience, which included his mother and Daphne, bewitched.

"Dickens certainly makes Old England come alive," Eleanor, sitting on his other side, suggested.

Miffed by Vera's multiple rebukes, he felt no guilt in taking notice of Eleanor. Let Vera make a fool of herself, for all he cared. He had tried enough times to rescue her. Let her wallow in her own folly.

Raleigh sent Eleanor what he knew to be his most devastating smile. "Yes, Dickens certainly does make Old England come alive. It's almost as though he lived through it himself."

"You are too witty." Eleanor's chest shook with laughter.

He could see by her unabashed response that her amusement was sincere, not an act to convince him that he was oh so charming. Her sincerity endeared her to him even more than she already had. In fact, he hadn't planned on becoming her defender that evening. What did he care if Flint wanted to make a remark or two about women's frivolities? Yet when Eleanor's face showed that she didn't take kindly to his observations, Raleigh found himself stepping in. And then later with Vera, he boosted Eleanor with more compliments—sentiments he suddenly realized he meant in all seriousness. What was happening to him?

As they talked about nothing and everything, reluctantly allowing themselves to be interrupted by other dinner guests when they cared to join the discussion, Raleigh studied Eleanor. Her beautiful brown eyes sparkled in the candlelight. He hadn't noticed before how random strands of red shone amid her auburn tresses. Her voice sounded to him like a pleasant melody, expressing high-minded ideas. No matter what plans his mother may or may not have had for the evening, he knew one thing: The threat of Flint, weak as it turned out to be, had left him with no uncertain feelings.

He was falling in love with the beautiful seamstress.

&a

"Oh, Eleanor, I can't believe what a night I had." Aunt Daphne's voice filled the foyer.

"Shhh, Aunt Daphne," Eleanor cautioned. "You'll wake the servants."

"Let them wake up. Let them share in my happiness." Aunt Daphne clasped her hands and stared at the ceiling, although Eleanor could see from her vacant expression that her mind wasn't focused on the wainscoting.

"Oh, Aunt Daphne, it was only a dinner party. Surely you couldn't have fallen madly in love with a strange man over the course of one evening."

"But oh, what courses they were!" Aunt Daphne noted. "Escargot, fruit and cheese, lobster bisque, salmon, vegetable salad, crown rack of lamb and potatoes, then a fine dessert of fresh berries and cream." She sighed.

Eleanor recalled the feast with no small amount of delight herself. "Yes, they were. I do believe that was the most splendid meal I have ever experienced. And the company and conversation were even more delightful." A picture of Raleigh popped into her head. She didn't urge it to leave.

"Ah, yes," Aunt Daphne agreed. "Mr. Flint Jarvis is such an extraordinary man!"

Flint Jarvis? Oh, yes. Reality brought Eleanor's mind home. "I could see you thought so. And so could everyone else."

"Is that so?" Aunt Daphne turned her nose skyward. "Let them see."

"Let them see, eh?" Eleanor tilted her nose at her aunt. "And let them talk, too?"

"And let them talk." Aunt Daphne's voice didn't seem as strong, and her head returned to its normal position.

"What about Vera?"

"Vera, indeed. I saw how she flirted with Flint." Aunt Daphne shrugged. "But all's fair in love and war."

"But what about her feelings? She's so shy and sheltered."

"Can you say that ten times very quickly?"

"Joke all you like, but—"

"She's not my client," Aunt Daphne snapped.

"Speaking of clients, does Mr. Jarvis know you're a seamstress?"

"Of course. Why do you ask?"

Eleanor shrugged. "He made a disparaging remark about women's frivolous dresses, a remark that Raleigh rebuffed."

"Oh, you know Flint and his dry wit."

Eleanor tried again. "Dry wit to you, but I do believe Vera's interest in him is serious."

Aunt Daphne's lips twisted, showing that Eleanor's chastisement had not fallen on deaf ears. "I'm not worried about Vera. I've known her ever since she became Mrs. Alden's companion five years ago. She has no other ambition."

Eleanor crossed her arms over her chest. "Is that what you really think? Or what you only hope?"

"Why. . .why," she stammered, "Vera and I can't be compared. We're so. . .so different."

"Yes. She is much younger than you are, I'm afraid. Much closer to Mr. Jarvis's age, perhaps?"

Aunt Daphne sniffed. "I'll have you to know that I am very well preserved for my age."

"That is even worse—if you are, indeed, older than you appear."

"How can you even think of speaking to me with such insolence?"

"I beg your deepest indulgence," Eleanor hastened to apologize. "It's just that. . .well. . .people like to talk when gentlemen pay court to ladies a bit older themselves."

"And you think that's what happened here?"

"I confess, I do." Eleanor decided not to be more specific and mention the others' observations.

Aunt Daphne shot her a mean look.

"Forgive me. But if I am not honest with you, who will be?"

"Dear, dear girl. I suppose you are right." A light of worry fell upon her face. "Did I really behave as badly as all that?"

"Oh, no, Aunt Daphne. I would never say that you behaved badly."

"Really?"

"Really."

Aunt Daphne let out a large sigh. "I suppose a confession is in order. I thought you were the one I would have offended tonight, if I offended anyone."

"Me? Don't be ridiculous."

"Then Mrs. Alden's plan must not have been as obvious as I told her I thought it would be." Aunt Daphne paused.

Plan? Eleanor remained silent, knowing that her aunt wouldn't be able to resist filling the stillness with the sound of her voice.

"Mrs. Alden thought that Mr. Jarvis would be quite taken with you."

Eleanor didn't know how to respond. "I suppose I should be flattered. Mr. Jarvis is obviously a popular man." A popular bon vivant, indeed. But he had impressed her not in the least. Raleigh, the man she had seen time and time again in circumstances nothing short of ordinary, was the one who had captured her heart.

"Yes, Flint is quite popular," her aunt agreed, bringing Eleanor back to the present.

"But why would Mrs. Alden care about my romantic prospects?" Eleanor asked.

Aunt Daphne opened her mouth, then shut it just as quickly. A moment passed before she decided to respond. "Never mind. As I said, all's fair in love and war. I wasn't in favor of meddling before, and I'm certainly not in favor of trying my hand at matchmaking again. But I do want your assurances: You are not interested in Mr. Jarvis in the least, are you?"

"Certainly not. I have no interest in him. I gather from your query that you plan to encourage him?"

"Indeed, I do." Aunt Daphne patted Eleanor's hand. "But don't you worry a bit. Knowing you, I'm sure you can content yourself with your Bible as a companion until the Lord sends someone else."

So she hadn't noticed Raleigh's attention toward her. Eleanor had a feeling that Aunt Daphne's lack of observation was for the best. "Let us retire, shall we? The time to awaken tomorrow morning to prepare for church will be here all too soon," Eleanor pointed out. "Good night, Aunt Daphne."

"Good night."

Eleanor headed up the stairs, eager to be alone, so she could contemplate the evening's events. Funny, the mysterious Flint Jarvis had turned out not to be so fascinating after all. Rather dull, in her eyes. Yet he enthralled all the others. Eleanor wondered how he could be so gallant and dress in such fine clothing if, indeed, he held an insignificant job. Slim evidence that something was amiss, but Eleanor didn't like where her instincts were taking her. She had to find out more about the mysterious Flint Jarvis before her aunt could be hurt. And she knew just where to begin.

eight

Eleanor felt a twinge of nervousness on her way to the Alden house. Was she being silly in telling Raleigh about her aunt's unmitigated attraction to Flint Jarvis?

She suppressed a sigh of exasperation. Ever since they had returned from the party, Aunt Daphne had spoken of nothing but Mr. Jarvis. Eleanor could distract her briefly by commenting on the dresses everyone wore, but the conversation would soon turn back to the world traveler.

Eleanor wished nothing more than for her aunt to be happy—even to see the world and leave Eleanor behind to hold down the business—if, and only if, the man she chose as a companion was worthy of her. And Eleanor was not at all sure that Mr. Jarvis fit the bill.

She remembered Mr. Jarvis and shuddered. He kept his audience of men and women alike enraptured with tales of exotic journeys, assuring them from time to time of his reluctance to boast. Eleanor grimaced. Reluctant? He hadn't stopped bragging the entire evening. The only time he seemed reticent was when one of the men asked how he managed to tear himself away from his occupation for months at a time so he could take long vacations. Then his mouth clamped shut more tightly than a house shuttered in anticipation of a hurricane.

As she disembarked from the carriage, she realized she wouldn't have to knock on the door. She spied Raleigh sitting on a lawn chair near a magnolia tree, looking over some papers. Her heart pounded. An unbidden image of what life with Raleigh would be like popped into her head. She could see herself walking across the freshly manicured lawn under a cloudless sky of blue, bringing him lemonade and cookies—lemonade she had squeezed with her own hands and cookies that smelled of fresh cinnamon and that had been baked with her love.

A second image of him entering the house after a hard day at court came into focus. He would breeze through the front doorway and head without hesitation to the drawing room, where Eleanor would be awaiting his arrival. She would be ready with coffee that had just been brewed, its bracing odor filling the room with a hospitable air. The evening paper would be folded so that his favorite section was immediately readable. His slippers would be ready for his tired feet. She had never seen his slippers, but she imagined them to be fashioned of black kid leather. Once he was settled, they would exchange accounts of their days, relishing one another's company.

Her daydreaming led to her steps slowing their pace. Perhaps dawdling was for the best, since she didn't want to appear too eager to see him.

He looked up from his papers and eyed her, pleasure evident in his expression. He rose from his seat and ambled toward her. "Eleanor!" he cried as soon as he was within earshot. "What brings you here on this fine day?"

The sound of his voice reminded her of a delightful symphony. And if she could judge by his rapt expression, he seemed glad to see her, too.

She swallowed and wished she had thought to drape a piece of cloth or two in the crook of her arm so she could appear to be on business. As it was, surely she appeared rather bold to be visiting as though she were an intimate of the family. Then again, she wished she could talk to Vera to gain knowledge of her account of the party. Perhaps she could at that. Yes, that would be an excellent excuse.

For now, she had been pressed to answer a query from

Raleigh. She would never admit she was glad to see him, despite the fact that she was. "I thought I might see Vera."

He grinned. "You want a full accounting of her version of the dinner party, eh?"

"And they say men don't understand women in the least," she teased.

"I claim no special understanding of the minds of ladies," he said, "but I can make an educated guess from time to time."

"Speaking of the party, my aunt certainly considers it the social event of the season."

He chuckled. "I'm not so sure anyone else would give our little soiree such a grand title, but I'm glad to hear she enjoyed herself. I trust you did, as well?" His voice held a question of hope.

"Yes, yes, indeed. The food was outstanding, and the conversation even more so, present company included." Realizing she had been too forward, she cast her gaze downward. At that moment, she noticed that the Aldens' lawn looked exceptionally green, much greener than the others nearby. Or was she imagining the degree of its emerald sparkle?

"I agree."

The soft tone of his voice encouraged her to look into his face. He was just as handsome under the unforgiving glare of sunshine as he had appeared amid flickering flames of beeswax candles, a condition that tended to flatter even the craggiest skin. But he looked just as vigorous, his complexion as healthy, his hair as shiny in broad daylight. Perhaps even more so.

"You do?" she blurted.

"Yes, I enjoyed the company and conversation immensely." His blue eyes took on a gentle light, and his voice remained low in volume. He moved just a bit closer to her.

Unable to form an intelligent response, she inwardly

blamed her sudden awkwardness on the spicy bay rum scent he wore. She resisted the desire to clear her throat—an action that would make a grating, unladylike sound that was sure to prove unappealing.

"Oh, yes. Our conversation," he said, "I remember now. I promised to loan you my copy of *Romeo and Juliet.*"

"Oh, yes. Yes, you did. I look forward to reading that. I do hope to see it performed someday."

"Baltimore is a big and important city that attracts people of high culture. I'm sure a traveling company will soon visit, and we can see it then. Or even a local production may be staged at some point."

Was he inviting her to see the play with him? She hid her anticipation under a bland mask. Surely issuing an invitation to an indefinite event at an unspecified date in the far future was simple—and noncommittal—enough that he could take the leap with little risk.

"Perhaps," she agreed. "But in the meantime, I assure you I have plenty of entertainment with my aunt at present."

"Oh?"

She swallowed. "Ever since she got back from the dinner party, all she can talk about is Mr. Flint Jarvis."

"Really?" He glanced at the empty, wrought-iron lawn chairs and gestured toward them. "Please, won't you sit with me for a moment? Unless Vera is expecting you at a certain time, that is."

"No. No, she isn't," Eleanor had to admit. She decided to take him up on his offer to seat herself in spite of the fact that the wrought-iron chairs weren't especially inviting. Since they were situated under an oak, she glanced at the portion where her dress would touch to be sure the fabric wouldn't encounter any outdoor debris. Only after she was satisfied that her garment would remain pristine did she sit.

"Do tell me about your aunt. You can trust me to keep anything you say in confidence."

Eleanor had visited with all intent of unabashedly sharing her concerns with Raleigh, but now that she was with him, the reality that she could be construed as betraying her aunt weighed on her mind. She hesitated.

"Come now, my dear. Aren't we the greatest of friends by now?"

My dear. There was that name again—a sweet nothing that nevertheless sent a pleasant shiver through her. She knew she had to speak with caution, lest she reveal too much. "Yes, I do feel we have a wonderful friendship. I am quite honored by that fact."

"On the contrary, I am the one who enjoys the honor."

She had watched carefully for any hint of deception in his voice or face but found none. She couldn't help but marvel at the fact that the man whom her aunt had found so distastefully cheap was now her friend—possibly her best friend here in Baltimore. She watched Raleigh settle back into his chair as much as a body is able to settle on unyielding wrought iron. She could see that he wasn't about to pressure her into voicing any observation against her will.

Eleanor took a moment to collect her thoughts. She inhaled, the gesture bringing to her attention the fresh scent of the evenly clipped grass. Noticing that the azalea bushes underneath the front windows of the house had lost their blooms, she wondered what color they would produce come next spring. In the meantime, floppy white petunias had made their appearance along the sides of the walkway. She peered at the white fence that blocked from view a generous vegetable garden, which consumed much of the side and backyards. Oh, to enjoy such space, with enough room to sow such a variety of plant life!

She glanced at Raleigh and noticed he wasn't even looking at her. Instead, he seemed to be making similar observations. She wondered how much he could really appreciate the yard when he had grown up in this house.

The realization that she couldn't linger all day struck her. *Lord, let me speak to Raleigh, whom I know to be Thy fellow servant, with wisdom. Let the purity of my motives be apparent. May Raleigh's response be led by Thy wisdom, as well. I submit my petition to Thee humbly and in the name of Thy Son, Jesus Christ. Amen.*

She spoke, the sound of her voice breaking into the stillness. "Raleigh."

He looked upon her, his comely features filled with kindness. "Yes?"

"I hope you realize that I do not mean to gossip, and certainly I do not intend to make any but the most flattering observation about my own aunt. I only mention her infatuation because I worry so about her."

He leaned toward her. "You worry? I must say, I find your concern rather charming. She took care of herself for many years before your arrival. I have the impression that she can continue to take care of herself now."

"Perhaps, but I have a feeling she has never encountered anyone like Mr. Jarvis in the past. She has spoken of nothing but him ever since the party, and her ramblings have become quite tiresome, I hate to say."

He chuckled. "I'm not at all sure that a little flirtation at a social function is anything to fret about."

"I think she considers it more than a flirtation," Eleanor confided. "I'm afraid she is in love after just one evening, and I suspect she is not being overconfident. I suspect her feelings are returned."

"And what if they are? I'm sure your aunt will see to it that you are always well taken care of. And you told me yourself that your father in Louisiana is concerned about your welfare above anything else." He allowed his gaze to catch hers. "Although if I may be so bold, your absence would cause the city of Baltimore to lose much of its sparkle."

"How you do talk, Raleigh." She clutched her fingers around her lace fan until she became conscious of each rib. Considerable restraint was needed to keep her from employing it to good use. "Please understand that I am not concerned about myself."

"I believe you. In fact, your involvement with others is one of your most endearing qualities."

Eleanor wasn't used to such flattery. This time, she decided a good whiff of fresh air was what she needed. She extended her fan and waved it as casually as she could, considering how her heart fluttered. "I do have some reservations about Mr. Jarvis." She hesitated. "I never should have mentioned this to you. You are my friend, but you are also his friend, after all. I am putting you in a most unfair position even to express the least bit of concern. Forget I ever said anything. I beg your deepest indulgence. If you'll excuse me, I'll be on my way." She rose from her seat.

He followed suit. "No, no. Please. I'm the one who should be asking your deepest pardon, and, indeed, I do. Please, feel free to speak with the utmost frankness. What is your worry, and how might I be of assistance in easing your mind?"

Eleanor took in a breath and looked into his eyes to search for his real feelings. His expression was kind, and he really did seem to be concerned along with her. "All right, then. I saw the look of interest in Mr. Jarvis's eyes as he held court with my aunt. There was no denying it."

"Surely that doesn't surprise you. Anyone can see that your aunt is still a beautiful woman."

"Agreed. But to my way of thinking, Mr. Jarvis puts on far too many airs. And he seems far too wealthy for a man who claims to hold an insignificant position in the wharf district."

"Is that what he claims? That his position is not one of significance? I would find that hard to believe myself."

"So you don't know exactly what he does for a living?"

"He mentioned in passing that he's in shipping. I must explain."

"Oh. I see." So he didn't know as much as Eleanor had thought. Still, now that she had broached the topic, she had to press on or abandon the subject forever. "But can't the term *shipping* mean almost anything here in Baltimore? Why, what if he's a smuggler?" She clenched her fists at the thought.

"A smuggler?" Raleigh's laugh echoed against the tree trunks and back. "What an imagination you have. What type of books did you say you used to read back in Louisiana?"

Eleanor bristled. "You know only too well." Recovering her composure, she continued. "I know that not every man is honorable."

"But Eleanor, if we accused every man who works at the wharf of being a smuggler, then half of Baltimore would be thrown in jail tonight."

"True," she conceded. "But you can't tell me exactly what he does. Have you ever handled any of his financial affairs as his lawyer so you would know for certain?"

"No, I can't say that I have."

"And you have never witnessed him at his office."

"No, but why would I? I have no concerns in the shipping business."

"So, then, he could be doing anything, and you wouldn't know about it. Why, he could even be a thief—or worse—and you would be completely in the dark."

Raleigh didn't answer for a moment. He tightened his lips and stared forward, his eyes adopting a blank light as though they looked but didn't observe what they were seeing. "I suppose."

"I have grown fond of Aunt Daphne since my arrival, and I would be loathe to see her begin to keep company with a man of ill repute."

"As would I. But what do you recommend that I do about it?"

"Could you find it in your heart to investigate further? Just to ease my mind and to protect my aunt. After all, she is more than just a seamstress to your dear mother. Anyone can see that Mrs. Alden is quite fond of Aunt Daphne."

"I won't deny that. But to poke my nose into another man's affairs, where it doesn't belong. . ." His lips twisted into an uncertain line. "You're asking me to take an awfully big risk."

"You have many important clients. I'm sure you know how to poke and prod without being observed."

He didn't answer right away but peered into her eyes. Sensing that to do anything else would make her seem less than determined, she returned his stare. Not for the first time, she noticed the purity of the color in his irises. They caught the light like jewels.

"You have such a pretty face," he observed.

I do? The fact that he was willing to express himself in such a way made her wish she could dance without seeming foolish.

He cleared his throat. "And with such beauty, you need not worry about business."

Her feet, which had felt so light an instant ago, now seemed to be immersed in concrete. Did Raleigh, seemingly such an astute and modern man, think she was dumb just because she was a woman? "How dare you!"

"I beg your pardon, I didn't mean—"

"Don't try to wriggle out of this one," she insisted. "I know exactly what you mean. You don't need to patronize me, Raleigh Alden! I am more than a pretty face. I'm as smart as any man. Maybe even smarter than some." Another thought occurred to her. "I can't help but wonder why you are so unwilling to help me, considering all that my aunt means to your mother."

And how much I had once hoped I meant to you.

Digging her heel into the ground in hopes of gaining

enough confidence not to wither, she added, "Perhaps you're so reticent to make a few casual inquiries about your friend Flint Jarvis because you are the one with something to hide."

"Something to hide? Me? Never!" he exclaimed. "How can you even suggest such a foolish thing?"

Deciding that she would be better off if she let Raleigh's newly awakened ire work in her favor, Eleanor didn't answer.

"I'll show you I have nothing to hide. And neither does Flint. I'm sure of it."

"Good. Then you can truly relish the sweet victory of proving me wrong."

"Sweet victory, indeed," he said. "Yes, it will be sweet. I have no need to tolerate such an insult. I will investigate Flint, if for no other reason than to show you just how mistaken you are."

&

Raleigh was so peeved by the time Eleanor departed that he hardly noticed that she had not ventured in to visit Vera as she had professed was her purpose. So she had come to see only him after all, to send him out to investigate Flint.

He remembered that he had neglected to get the book for her. Never mind. At least it offered him an excuse to see her again.

See her again? Why would he want to see such an irritable woman again? What was he thinking? How could his foolish heart betray him so? Why, Eleanor Kerr was by far the most exasperating, demanding, nosy, vexing, imaginative. . .romantic, beautiful, smart, stunning. . .

He let out a groan. He tried again to focus on her irksome qualities but to no avail. Her favorable qualities made themselves too apparent.

Raleigh thought back over their conversation. She hadn't been ruffled by his declaration that they were the greatest of friends. In fact, she seemed completely in agreement—certainly not displeased. But he realized that he wished their bonds surpassed acquaintanceship.

He would see her again, surely. He needed no fresh excuse, not after she demanded that he investigate Flint. And he knew she wouldn't rest until he came up with an answer for her—an answer that would satisfy her curiosity. She was a formidable presence when she chose to be, and she wouldn't be brushed off with a vague response.

He sighed. How had he let himself get sidelined into such a distasteful project?

Raleigh knew exactly how. He wanted to please Eleanor, even if it meant sticking his nose where it definitely didn't belong.

❧

Two weeks had passed, and Eleanor still hadn't heard from Raleigh. Even worse, Flint Jarvis had developed the habit of visiting unannounced—and uninvited, as far as she was concerned—almost every evening. The hours between dinner and bedtime, which Aunt Daphne once used to catch up on the day's sewing for clients, were now lost to endless flirtations as she sat in the parlor and listened to Mr. Jarvis tell of his adventures again and again.

At first Eleanor didn't mind so much. She found some pleasure in watching as Aunt Daphne giggled and fluttered her eyelashes at him. Eleanor watched the years melt away from her. But as Mr. Jarvis began to repeat his tales, embellishing them so that each adventure became grander and more dangerous, Eleanor wondered if he had lost his ability—or his desire—to distinguish fact from fiction.

One evening after a particularly long visit, Aunt Daphne led her into the sewing room so they could organize their projects for the next day. She chattered so much that Eleanor wondered if her aunt was accomplishing anything.

Finally, Eleanor summoned the nerve to confront her aunt.

"Aunt Daphne, don't you find it interesting how Mr. Jarvis changes his story just a wee bit with each retelling?"

Aunt Daphne set a pattern on her table. "Whatever do you mean?"

Eleanor swallowed. "Well, on Tuesday he said his last trip to Kansas City was quite ordinary. On Thursday he said he encountered bank robbers, but he merely witnessed the scene as police took them away; but today, he claimed to wrestle one of them down to the floor at risk to his own life."

"Yes, he does lead quite an exciting life, doesn't he?"

Eleanor sat at her seat and halfheartedly sorted through several spools of thread. "But wouldn't you think that he would have mentioned something that exciting on the first telling? After all, it isn't every day that one meets bank robbers. Not even in Kansas City."

"Indeed!" Aunt Daphne plopped in her chair, took out her fan, and waved it in front of her face, not in the coy manner she employed in front of Mr. Jarvis, but in the nonchalant way of a woman sincerely seeking to cool her face against the elements.

Her actions made Eleanor realize that she could be feeling a bit more fresh herself on such a heated summer evening. She withdrew her everyday fan of stiff cotton embellished with plain lace and fanned herself. Moving the hot air around helped to relieve her somewhat, although not nearly as much as she would have liked.

"Clearly we aren't concentrating on this work. It's too late, and we're too tired and excited. Perhaps I should make some lemonade," Eleanor suggested, hoping the gesture of friendship would cool off both their bodies and tempers. "Would you care for some?"

"Yes, I do believe I would."

The women rose and, after Aunt Daphne extinguished the lights, made the short journey to the kitchen. Once there,

Aunt Daphne reached for the lemons.

Eleanor shooed her away. "No, no. Allow me. You sit and rest."

Aunt Daphne took her up on her offer and situated herself in the chair the cook used when she took a short break or when she shelled peas or shucked corn. "Why don't you make enough for tomorrow night, as well? Flint seems to enjoy our lemonade."

Eleanor eyed the empty pitcher fashioned of clear glass, a reminder left from the evening. "Yes, he certainly does."

"Just so you are aware, he will be stopping by tomorrow evening in time to take me to dinner. I gave Cook the night off. You won't object to getting supper on your own, will you?"

"Of course not."

"I'm sure you don't mind escaping from his stories," Aunt Daphne noted, "although I really don't think it's his storytelling that bothers you."

"I don't mind stories. But travel is only of passing interest to me, and I'm not accustomed to those who embellish their tales." Eleanor felt herself squeezing a defenseless lemon with more vigor than needed. The scent of the pulverized fruit enlivened her, yet made her feel more relaxed at the same time. She rescued a stray seed and placed it on the wooden counter.

"So you say." Aunt Daphne allowed a tense silence to hang in the air before she spoke again. "Why don't you tell me the real reason you are so opposed to my suitor. I know you're not the type to be jealous. Are you worried that if I marry, you won't have a job here any longer?" Aunt Daphne asked. "If that's your concern, think nothing more of it. You have proven yourself to be a fine seamstress. Why, I do believe that you could open up your own shop if you set your mind to it."

"I have no such desire," Eleanor promised as she washed the glass pitcher, being careful not to damage the hand-painted daisies on its front.

"Good." She smiled. "For if you did, you just might prove to be entirely too much competition for your old aunt."

"Oh, really, how you do go on." Though Eleanor's observation was made in a frivolous tone, she felt flattered. Aunt Daphne was not one to dispense compliments easily, at least not to anyone who wasn't a client.

"If you're not worried about the business, then what?" Aunt Daphne pressed.

Eleanor hesitated. She wished the conversation hadn't progressed to such a point, but now that they had begun, she was obliged to finish. If she didn't, Eleanor sensed that her aunt would never allow her to visit the topic of her courtship with Mr. Jarvis in the future. "It's so difficult for a woman who lives alone with no one to look out for her best interests and well-being."

Aunt Daphne shrugged. "I don't find it especially difficult. I suppose I'm accustomed to being alone. I have learned to trust my judgment and intuition."

"Your trust is not misplaced, no doubt," Eleanor hastened to assure her as she mixed lemon juice and sugar together. "But even the most brilliant among us can be blinded by emotion."

"You feel that I am blinded by emotion?" The edgy tone of her aunt's voice left Eleanor feeling nervous.

"It's not entirely impossible, is it?" She stopped her work and turned to her aunt. She walked a few paces to her chair, knelt, and clasped her aunt's hands in hers. "Oh, Auntie, I'm so happy for you. I do so love to see you enjoying Mr. Jarvis's company. But I don't wish to see you become involved with someone who isn't worthy of you."

"I'm glad you hold me in such high esteem. Only, why wouldn't a wealthy man who travels the world be worthy of me?"

She squeezed her aunt's hands. "That's just it. Where does he get his wealth? Has he discussed it with you?" Eleanor knew her voice betrayed her hope.

"No. Of course not. Most men don't discuss their business affairs with their wives, much less with women they are courting." Aunt Daphne took her hands from Eleanor's, although to Eleanor's relief, the gesture was bereft of rudeness or anger.

Eleanor rose to her feet. "I'm sure he'll want to know all about your business. That will be a jolt for you, won't it? Having to share everything with a man?"

"He doesn't seem to place a great deal of curiosity in my business affairs. I find that fact rather comforting, in a way. His lack of curiosity only proves that he isn't interested in me for whatever income I can bring to his household. Besides, what man of his station would want his wife to maintain a business once they are—" She stopped herself short.

"*If* they are?" Eleanor didn't look her aunt in the face as she added water to the juice and sugar.

"I mean," Aunt Daphne stumbled, "if we ever are. . .uh. . .if we ever take our visitations beyond courtship."

Eleanor stopped stirring the lemonade in midcircle. "Has he proposed?"

"No, but I think he will. And I think I might accept."

"Aunt Daphne!"

"Oh, do be happy for me, won't you, dear heart? It would make things ever so much more pleasant."

Eleanor watched the lemonade settle. She braced herself before looking into her aunt's face. "Of course, I will support any decision you make in any way I know possible."

"Thank you, Eleanor."

Eleanor poured two glasses of lemonade without speaking. Raleigh had to come through for her. He just had to!

Father in heaven, I pray that Thou wilt keep my aunt in Thy care. I pray that I am wrong about Mr. Jarvis. But whether I'm wrong or right, please allow me to find out before it's too late.

nine

Raleigh was about to leave his office for a court session when he heard a knock on the door.

"Not now, Monroe," he called with enough vigor to be heard through the heavy oak. "I have no time to tarry."

Monroe nevertheless stepped just inside the door. "I beg your pardon, sir, but it's Eustis. He said he has the information you want, sir."

Eustis. Finally. It had taken him long enough. Raleigh set the court brief on his desk and consulted his gold pocket watch. He had exactly nineteen minutes before he would be forced to leave or risk being late for court. "All right. Send him in."

Eustis entered, hat in hand. "Good mornin', Mr. Raleigh."

"Good morning, Eustis." A glimpse of the man before him confirmed that he had chosen the right person. Eustis wasn't particularly handsome, and he was dressed in a style plain enough to blend in with dockworkers. "I don't mean to be short with you, but I have very little time. Please be brief."

"Yes, sir. I poked around as much as I could without stirring up any trouble. I didn't find out much. Maybe not as much as you would have liked."

Raleigh hid his disappointment with a nod. "I understand that you had to sacrifice for the sake of discretion. No one has any idea that you are working for me in this capacity, do they?"

"No, sir. I was careful."

"Good." Normally Raleigh would have sat back in his chair and offered a seat to Eustis, but he omitted the courtesy because of the shortage of time. "So tell me what you were able to discover."

"Mr. Jarvis has an office near Pier 7, but no matter when I stop by, day or night, he never seems to be there."

"Really? Then where is he?" Raleigh tried not to fist his hands. "Were you able to find out anything?"

"He seems to have a fine old time around town, Mr. Raleigh. He goes about in fine style, eating at the best dining establishments with all sorts of friends—fine lookin' gentlemen." He shoved his hands in his pants pockets and rattled what sounded like a few coins. "Why, I think you even ate with him one day yourself, Mr. Raleigh."

"I can't deny that." Raleigh had made deliberate plans to share a meal with the dapper Flint in hopes of deflecting suspicion from himself should Flint find out that someone—specifically Raleigh himself—was digging into his business. "You say he had other dinner companions this week?"

"Yes, sir. He dined twice with Miss Daphne Kerr, the seamstress who runs a shop out of her home on Cathedral Street."

"Yes." Conscious that he needed to depart soon, Raleigh picked up the court brief and held it in the crook of his arm. "She is the only female companion you noticed?"

"Yes, sir. He don't seem to pay other women any mind."

Raleigh knew his eyebrows shot up in surprise. He reset his features into a blank expression as soon as he could. "Thank you, Eustis. You have done a fine job for me. I'll remember that."

"Thank you, Mr. Raleigh." He tipped his hat and made his exit.

Raleigh was left with an uneasy feeling. Judging from the account he had just heard, Flint didn't sound as though he was gainfully employed. Perhaps Eleanor had a right to be suspicious, after all.

⁂

The following day, Eleanor arrived at the Alden home, thankful that Vera had sent word that she wanted a new housedress sewn. She had begged off making a firm appointment, truth-fully pleading a full schedule already, then made a point of waiting until just before dinner to arrive in hopes that Raleigh would be back from court. If she met him, she could pull him aside and ask what, if anything, he had discovered about the mysterious Flint Jarvis.

She knocked on the door, but Monroe didn't answer. How unusual. She couldn't remember a time when he wasn't haunting the doorway. Since she was expected for her appointment, Eleanor pushed the door open and entered. She darted her gaze around the room and tried not to seem too obvious as she looked for Raleigh. At first she didn't see him anywhere. Her heart felt as though it had sunk into her toes. She tried to tell herself the feeling was merely the result of wanting to learn about Flint Jarvis, but she knew better. She welcomed any excuse to visit with Raleigh.

Father in heaven, I pray that Thou hast forgiven me for my rudeness to Raleigh the last time we spoke. I shouldn't have let my anger get the best of me. I should not have given in to the temptation to bait him with a challenge so he would bend to my will and do my bidding. Lord, no matter what happens today, let me be conscious of Thy will, not my own. In the name of Thy Son, amen.

Eleanor took in a breath and straightened her posture, determined that her visit would be a success on all fronts. Perhaps if she dawdled with Vera, she would be able to linger until Raleigh returned.

She headed up to Mrs. Alden's bedroom, where Vera was sure to be found.

"I just don't know what to do about Vera."

Eleanor stopped. That was Raleigh's voice! The door to the bedroom was ajar, and she could hear him speaking.

"She certainly made a fool of herself at the dinner party," he continued.

The dinner party? Why was he talking about the dinner party? That had happened more than two weeks ago. And how had Vera made a fool of herself? Eleanor had to know! She stopped short so she could listen.

Mrs. Alden's voice filtered into the foyer. "I must agree, Raleigh. I had no intention of Vera taking any interest in Mr. Jarvis. When I saw her flirting wildly with him, I couldn't believe my eyes."

Eleanor knew she was being impolite to eavesdrop. Listening to this conversation went against every good thing she had been taught. But she couldn't resist. Obviously, Vera was out on some mysterious errand, or they never would be talking about her in such a way.

"Good," Raleigh said. "So you'll understand when I say that if you have any regard for Vera or Daphne, you'll cut off all ties with anyone having connections with Flint, including Miss Jessica."

"Jessica! But she has been my friend for years. I will not cut off communications with her." A moment of silence ensued before she added, "Jessica is not her nephew's guardian. She is not to be blamed for his actions. Although I do confess, I'm disappointed that all did not go as planned."

"Go as planned?" Surprise was evident in Raleigh's voice.

Careful not to make a peep, Eleanor brought her ear as closely as she could to the open door without being seen.

"Yes." Silence filled the room. Knowing Mrs. Alden as well as she did, Eleanor could imagine disgust with Raleigh's obtuseness registering on her face. "Didn't you suspect?"

"Suspect what?"

Mrs. Alden exhaled. "I wonder how someone as smart as you are can be so dense at times. Well, I suppose I might as well confess. Daphne and I had hoped that Eleanor, not Vera and Daphne, would take an exceptional interest in Mr. Jarvis."

"Eleanor?"

"Yes. I had hoped she would find herself to be an excellent match for him."

Eleanor tensed and watched Raleigh's face. Would his expression reveal his feelings for her?

"Daphne betrayed me, really," Mrs. Alden confided to her son. "When we discussed the party earlier, she said she was in complete agreement that Flint and Eleanor would go well together."

"The poor girl has only been here a couple of months, and already Daphne wants to marry her off?" Raleigh asked.

"I assure you, Daphne only has Eleanor's best interests at heart."

"But the sewing business—"

"I'm sure she thought that while Flint made his way abroad, Eleanor would stay in town and help her hold down the shop."

Eleanor felt her mouth twitch. Mrs. Alden knew Aunt Daphne too well.

"Mother, I can see why Daphne might be concerned about her own niece, but why would you be concerned with Eleanor's romantic affairs?"

She paused. "Because. . .because. . .never you mind. There shall be no argument, Raleigh." His mother's voice was stern. "I have a notion as to why you want to cut Flint off from us. You are jealous."

"Jealous?" Raleigh blurted. "Don't be preposterous. I am not jealous of anyone."

"Indeed, you're not? I think you protest too much, Raleigh. Everyone at the party could see that you have developed great feelings for Eleanor."

Eleanor nearly gasped with delight. So Raleigh's feelings had become obvious to his mother! Surely he would soon be making his intentions known to her, as well. A smile tickled her lips, and her foot began to tap as though she could break out into a waltz. With a show of self-control, she kept a happy sigh to herself.

"Really?" Raleigh protested. "I don't see how anyone can say that."

His words brought Eleanor back down to earth and then some. How could an utterance of just one sentence take her emotions from the heights of a mountain to the depths of a well?

"Is that so?" Mrs. Alden challenged him. "Then may I ask, whom are you trying to fool: me or yourself?"

"I—I . . ."

Eleanor could almost hear Mrs. Alden smiling. "Do you mean we sent you to Virginia and paid tuition to the law school of William and Mary all those years just so you could become tongue-tied in front of your own mother? I hardly see how you could be doing your professors proud."

A slight pause ensued, during which Eleanor imagined Raleigh drawing himself up to his full height. "Mother, you must admit, you are more intimidating than any of my professors ever were—and even most judges."

Eleanor suppressed a giggle.

"That's a fine excuse, but I will have none of that." Mrs. Alden's firm voice only proved Raleigh's observation. "Rather than meddling in the love affairs of others, I suggest that you make your intentions known to Eleanor."

Eleanor held back a gasp. So Raleigh really did have feelings for her! His mother had just admitted it, right to his face. If she could see through him, then her instincts hadn't led her astray. Again she experienced a sudden lightness of foot. She could almost imagine her toes lifting off the floor so she could float in midair.

"But I don't wish to make my intentions known to Eleanor, as you put it. You may think I have feelings for her, and I do. I am quite fond of her as a charming and beautiful companion for conversation about books and such."

Eleanor's emotions churned. The words *charming* and *beautiful*—words she had seldom heard to describe her—roiled through her head, only to be superceded by the lukewarm phrase *companion for conversation,* a term that could have applied to almost any acquaintance.

Eleanor felt her lips tighten. Yes, he had admitted a tepid partiality to her not so long ago. She couldn't accuse him of dishonesty. And what more did she have a right to ask? He hadn't mentioned courting her. How could she consider him a suitor? She shook her head. Such thoughts, running wild as they were, left her unsettled. How far had she let her feelings for him go? Too far. She tightened her grip on the fabric samples she held, conscious yet uncaring that the motion would wrinkle them.

"I believe your feelings for her run deeper than friendship," Mrs. Alden said.

Eleanor felt her pulse increase as she stopped breathing for a split second. She pressed her head against the wall by the door in anticipation of his response.

"Believe what you like," Raleigh answered, "but I have never considered Eleanor as someone I might like to court."

Eleanor clutched the woolen fabric samples even tighter, sorely testing their durability. In her heart, she couldn't be surprised by his response, but disappointment filled her nonetheless.

"And why ever not?" Mrs. Alden grilled him. "She is certainly pretty enough."

A rush of pleasure permeated Eleanor, even though the compliment was uttered by an older woman.

"I won't deny that she does have a pretty face and pleasant figure."

So he had noticed! The feeling of delight was joined by a rise of heat to Eleanor's face, making her grateful for the dimness in the empty hallway.

"And she sews a fine seam," Mrs. Alden added.

"She sews a fine seam, yes, but would she have the knowledge or experience—or even the desire—to take on the responsibilities of a lawyer's wife?" Raleigh asked.

Wife? Wife!

Eleanor wanted to burst into the room and shout, "Yes! Yes! I have the desire, and what I don't know now about being a lawyer's wife, I can learn!" Instead, she forced herself to remain standing where she was.

"Raleigh, how can you doubt Eleanor? As your wife, she would have plenty of support from the household staff, and I certainly can tell her a thing or two about how to set a fine table."

"And why are you suddenly so eager to take on Eleanor as your daughter-in-law?" Raleigh's tone betrayed his doubt. "I had no notion that you wanted me to marry."

"Of course I do, for your happiness."

"Or for your happiness, Mother? I know Eleanor and Vera get along well. I suppose you think she could encourage Vera to stay on indefinitely as your companion?"

"I doubt Eleanor holds that kind of sway over Vera."

"But it's worth a try, isn't it? Especially since your attempts to distract Eleanor from me by throwing Flint her way failed. And now that you see the folly of your strategy, you are putting another plan into progress. Are you not?" He paused. Eleanor imagined that he used such techniques in the courtroom to stymie witnesses.

"How could you accuse me of such deviousness? Why, I had no idea you were developing a fondness for Eleanor until the night of the party."

"Is that so? I may have just returned to Baltimore after an extended absence, Mother, but I think I have an idea of how your mind works. Initially, you would have liked for me to become attached to Vera since she is from a good family. Then you would have been guaranteed that she would never leave this house. But when you saw that Vera simply doesn't pique my interest whether she's sitting by your bedside or dressed in a fabulous gown, you formulated another plan, a plan that would protect your interests should Vera eventually attract a suitor," he said. "You surmised that should I marry Eleanor, she would be so grateful to be your daughter-in-law that she would eagerly do your bidding for the remainder of your days. Am I right?"

"Now that's the kind of dramatic argument I would expect from a graduate of a fine Virginia school of law. I can almost hear the jury give a collective gasp and the court observers break out into whispers and expressions of shock."

"But am I right, Mother?" he persisted.

"Of course not." Mrs. Alden's voice sounded weak.

Eleanor crossed her arms. So Mrs. Alden wasn't the champion Eleanor thought. She was simply contriving to use her as a pawn to advance her own interests! Then she remembered Mrs. Alden's remarkable ability to rise from her bed to attend the dinner party. Of course, Mrs. Alden could do most anything she set her mind to. Had Eleanor not been one of the players manipulated on Mrs. Alden's stage, Eleanor could have granted her unbridled admiration.

Raleigh spoke once more. "I can't believe you chose Flint Jarvis of all people as a romantic prospect for any woman in whom you place any regard."

"And why is that?"

"His character is suspect."

"Whatever your accusations, I don't believe them. Flint Jarvis has always been a friend of yours. Are you implying that you have poor judgment in choosing friends?" With the subject changed, Mrs. Alden's voice took on new conviction.

"You exaggerate his importance to me, Mother. He was a

childhood classmate once upon a time but hardly one of my intimates."

"You didn't object to his being invited to the dinner."

"No, but at the time I was taking his connection to your friend Jessica into consideration, and I didn't know about his frivolous style of life," Raleigh observed.

"What do you mean by 'frivolous style of life'?"

Finally, the information she wanted to hear. Eleanor put aside her tumultuous emotions about her own circumstances long enough to crane her neck, so she could be sure not to miss a word. For Aunt Daphne's sake, she had to know about Mr. Jarvis. She felt her body tense.

"Since the party, it has come to my attention that Flint's source of wealth is not known. He says he is gainfully employed in shipping, yet he shows no evidence that such an enterprise supports his ability to gallivant about town every day."

"So he doesn't spend his time with his nose buried in legal briefs all day like you do." Eleanor could visualize Mrs. Alden shrugging. "Does that make him a villain?"

"I hope not."

"You may have influence in the courts, but I would think long and hard about accusing someone of wrongdoing if I were you." Eleanor imagined Mrs. Alden shaking her finger at Raleigh as she dispensed such advice.

"Indeed. And I assure you, I express my concerns to you in the strictest confidence." He exhaled. "I tell you once and for all, your best laid plans have failed. I am not interested in Vera, simply because she melts into the wall, nor am I interested in Eleanor, because though she is a fine seamstress, that is still her station—that of a tradeswoman."

Eleanor flinched.

"Raleigh! How dare you be such a snob! I thought I reared you to be better than that. You know how well I regard

Daphne, so why should I not extend the same feelings to her niece? Besides, I think Eleanor was born to a higher calling. You must remember that her family fell upon hard times through no fault of their own, darling."

"Yes, I know. But I have an image to maintain if you wish to remain in this fine home and to enjoy your current luxuries in life, Mother. Now let us not discuss this anymore."

Eleanor felt her eyes tearing. How could Raleigh, the man who had shown her only kindness, suddenly turn on her and act as though she was nothing more than an insignificant fool? Perhaps she was not insignificant, but at that moment, she felt quite foolish.

Eleanor knew she couldn't face Raleigh or anyone else who mattered to her. She spun on her heel and tiptoed through the hallway, down the stairs, and to the foyer. She looked beyond the muslin draperies out the window. Thankfully, the carriage still waited.

Monroe materialized in the foyer, seemingly out of thin air. "Miss Kerr. I'm sorry; I didn't know you were here. May I announce you to Mrs. Alden?"

"No, that won't be necessary."

"I'll tell her you're here," he insisted.

"No, I'm not here." Eleanor touched the doorknob to signal her imminent departure.

Monroe gave her a quizzical look.

"I mean, I'm here, but I need to go back. I won't be seeing anyone."

He furrowed his brow. "Are you quite sure?"

"Yes, yes. I—I left something at home. I'll be back another time." Had Eleanor still been a little girl, she would have held her hands behind her back, fingers crossed. But she had left something at home. Her pride.

As she rode toward Cathedral Street, she peered out of the carriage window as though she were seeing everything for the last time. And, indeed, she was. Or at least, that was the intent she felt by the time she reached the row house she had recently been calling home.

Once she disembarked, she rushed into the house. She had a mission, and that was to pack her bags.

"Eleanor?" Aunt Daphne called from the sewing room in the back of the house.

She composed herself, so her voice would be strong when she answered. "It is I." Eleanor made a beeline for the stairs, hoping she could escape before Aunt Daphne came in to interrogate her.

"That was a mighty short visit to the Aldens'." Aunt Daphne's voice was growing closer, and the *clacking* of her boot heels was becoming louder as she approached.

Eleanor hurried up the stairs. "Yes, ma'am."

"Is everything all right?"

Eleanor raced to her room, but she wasn't rapid enough. Aunt Daphne followed on her heels. Eleanor thought she seemed to move quickly for someone her age.

Aunt Daphne stood in the doorway. Eleanor had been unable to shut the door behind her without hitting her aunt in the nose. "Clearly, something is amiss. Tell me what happened. Was Vera unhappy with the patterns or the fabric you suggested? Do you want me to go by there and make amends?"

"No, Aunt Daphne. It's nothing like that. I didn't even see Vera. She was out." Eleanor threw the fabric samples onto her bed.

"Out? Out where? She never goes out."

Eleanor yanked her hat from her head. In her distraction, she forgot about her pearl-embossed hatpin, which made its presence known by scraping against the back of her head beside her chignon. Too upset even to utter an expression of pain, she searched for it with nimble fingers and pulled it out of her hair. "I have no idea where Vera was."

"Eleanor, you're not making sense."

She fiddled with the pin with such vigor that she nearly stuck her thumb. "You're right, Aunt Daphne, I'm not. In fact, nothing about this town makes any sense. I appreciate everything you've done for me, but I can't live here anymore. I'm leaving for Louisiana next week. And there's nothing you can do to stop me."

ten

"Eleanor! You don't mean that!" Aunt Daphne cried. "Surely you don't plan to go back to Louisiana. This is your home now. Baltimore." She swept her arm over Eleanor's modest bedroom as though it represented all of Charm City.

Following her aunt's hand with her gaze, Eleanor peered out of her smallish window decorated by fresh white cotton curtains. She crossed her arms, an impulsive gesture made to help her fight unwanted feelings. Indeed, she had become attached to the city and its people in the short time she had been a part of the fabric of their lives.

Taking in a deep breath, she noticed pleasant and not-so-pleasant city odors coming into her room through the open window: cooking aromas, horse manure, and coal smoke mingled with rotting kitchen waste, musky harbor smells, flowers, and the occasional tree. It all signified life to Eleanor. Her ears picked up the other element of life in the city: sounds. A constant drone was always present. She heard horses clopping and neighing, cart wheels rumbling, and people chattering, though she could rarely distinguish their words. The exceptions were peddlers—some of them boys rather than men—who shouted the names and qualities of their wares, so their voices penetrated the air.

When she first arrived in Baltimore, Eleanor had found the noises and scents unsettling. In Louisiana, she had lived in a neighborhood of spacious homes and generous lawns, far from the hum of the center of New Orleans. Here, she was situated in the middle of a vibrant life. Not only had she become accustomed to her busy surroundings, but she would surely miss them.

"I must admit, this city feels like home to me. But I'm afraid I must return to my father's house. The time has come." Though she kept confidence etched on her face as she regarded her aunt, Eleanor heard a wistful catch in her voice.

"Don't be absurd, child. You don't want to leave now. Think of how our business is booming. Orders for Christmas dresses are pouring in so fast that you and I put together will be hard pressed to fill them all. Think of the nice little nest egg you are building for yourself, with no one's toil but your own. Isn't that something to be proud of?"

"God has blessed me. But Aunt Daphne, I know you'll find someone else to replace me in plenty of time to fill all your orders and then some."

"Where can I find a seamstress as fine as you are on such short notice?" Aunt Daphne crossed her arms. "I'd have to train anyone else for months, and even then, she might prove not to have a whit of talent for sewing." She pointed her forefinger at her niece. "You're a natural, Eleanor."

Though Eleanor felt flattered, the pleasure of her aunt's rare compliment was deflated by her obvious self-interested motivation. Disappointment that her aunt's fondness was tinged with selfishness pricked at Eleanor's heart. "I'm sorry, Aunt Daphne, but—"

Aunt Daphne moved closer and placed her hands on Eleanor's shoulders. As her aunt moved, Eleanor could smell the faint but bland odor of the lavender sachet kept in her dresser drawers to freshen her clothes. Since arriving in Baltimore, Eleanor had come to associate the fragrance with her aunt. She had been surprised that such a vivacious woman had chosen a delicate scent, expecting her to favor lilac. But when Aunt Daphne reminded her that Eleanor's grandmother wore lavender, she understood that her wearing it was a form of remembrance.

"Please, Eleanor," Aunt Daphne said. "Think of your father. He only wanted you to come here for your health. You can't go back to Louisiana now and risk contracting malaria as your mother did. Certainly you don't wish to endure such pain as she did, even to the death."

"Of course not." Eleanor shuddered as she recalled her mother's suffering. "I wouldn't wish her type of death on anyone." She pulled away from Aunt Daphne's grasp and turned her back, so her aunt wouldn't see the tears that threatened.

"Then you see why you can't possibly go home now."

Eleanor wiped her tears away using as little arm movement as possible in hopes that her aunt wouldn't notice. "On the contrary, it's imperative that I return home now. I'll be fine." She held back a sniffle.

"You don't know that." Aunt Daphne's voice held the confidence of a woman firm in her conviction. And why shouldn't it? Eleanor knew her aunt was right.

Having composed herself, Eleanor turned back to face her aunt. "Perhaps I don't. But it's a chance I'm willing to take."

Aunt Daphne stepped closer. "How can you be so foolish with your life? Didn't the Reverend Marks preach just the other Sunday that the human body is a temple of God? Do you want to destroy your very temple?"

"Of course not. But remember, people live in Louisiana for a lifetime at the peak of health. I believe that Papa's reaction to my mother's illness by sending me here was a bit strong. Even you would agree." She didn't wait for her aunt to protest. "I—I just can't stay in a place where they talk about people behind their backs. That's all." To demonstrate her feelings, Eleanor needed only five paces to reach the oak wardrobe that stood against the north wall. She opened the door and surveyed her assortment of ten dresses and four pairs of shoes. Assessing them, she wondered if she should send the best ones in trunks to arrive ahead of her in Louisiana.

"What? Is that what this is about? A little bit of gossip?" Aunt Daphne's words came closer together. "What did you hear? Tell me."

Eleanor eyed the dress she wore the night of the dinner party, the dress that Raleigh seemed to find flattering on her figure. On the one hand, she wanted to enshrine it as a memory of the evening—the one night when she thought Raleigh could love her. On the other, she fought a real desire to cut it to shreds then and there.

Eleanor desperately wanted to quote St. Paul's admonitions about being a busybody, but since she had learned the news from eavesdropping, she felt that to chastise her aunt would be the height of hypocrisy.

"If you are looking for somewhere devoid of rumor and intrigue, then you will soon find you have no place to live at all. I know of nowhere on earth where gossip isn't present to some degree." Aunt Daphne chuckled.

Still silent, Eleanor fingered the skirt of the dress she had worn to the dinner party. Nothing her aunt said helped to ease the hurt of hearing what was said by Raleigh and Mrs. Alden when they thought she wasn't listening. Eleanor supposed she deserved what she got for eavesdropping. Why, if her dear mother were still alive, she would have dispensed a tongue-lashing that Eleanor would have never forgotten. The idea reminded her again of how much she missed her mother.

Eleanor forced herself to bring her mind back to the present, where she could see that she had no choice but to bring out the heavy artillery. She spun on the heel of her boot and looked her aunt straight in the eyes. "Maybe not, but you won't be so amused when you find out about whom Raleigh and Mrs. Alden were gossiping. Your very own Flint Jarvis."

All mirth evaporated from Aunt Daphne's face. "Really? I don't believe it."

"Believe it."

Eleanor watched her aunt swallow. "Why would they tell you anything about Flint?"

Eleanor squirmed but summoned her resolve to reveal the truth. "I overheard a conversation. I know I was wrong to eavesdrop, but—"

Aunt Daphne flitted her hand at Eleanor. "Never mind that. Some of the best tidbits are the ones overheard. Just tell me what they said."

Eleanor took in a breath. "Raleigh said that Flint's source of wealth is questionable."

"It is not." Aunt Daphne puffed herself up so that she brought to Eleanor's mind a miffed feline. "He's in shipping. What's questionable about that?"

"I don't know the details," Eleanor answered in all truthfulness, "but Raleigh was questioning his integrity. And if you're serious about becoming Mrs. Flint Jarvis, I think you should, too. For your own good."

"Well, I think he has some nerve! I can judge Flint for myself. I don't need anyone else to interfere. Besides, I think Raleigh is just jealous. Did you know that Flint is leaving next month on a trip to India?"

"No. I'm sure that will be quite exciting for him." Eleanor tried not to grimace at the thought of a fresh batch of stories to be repeated with increasing embellishment.

"It will be. And all the while, Raleigh will be working on dry legal issues here in Baltimore. As I said, he's just envious." Aunt Daphne wasn't finished. "And as for you, my dear niece, I do believe you're jealous, too."

A chuckle escaped Eleanor's lips. "Me? Jealous of Mr. Jarvis? Surely you know I have no desire to travel, although I'm happy for him that he has the opportunity since he obviously derives such joy from taking journeys around the world."

"I don't mean you're envious of his trips. I mean you are

envious of me. Here I have, without any effort, attracted the interest of a wealthy and worldly man, while you have not."

Aunt Daphne's comment stung her no less than a slap to the cheek. Eleanor wanted to blurt out that she and Raleigh were great friends, but decided that she was better off not mentioning anything about him at all.

"I know what you're thinking. You're thinking that you are successful because you have managed to pique the interest of Raleigh Alden."

Eleanor remained silent but tilted her chin skyward.

"And you're going to say that Raleigh is just as important and wealthy as Flint. Well, maybe he is, but I can't imagine that tightwad doing anything more exciting than visiting an ice-cream parlor." She wagged her finger at Eleanor. "And I'll bet he orders vanilla, too."

"I see nothing wrong with vanilla. It's a perfectly fine, solid flavor."

"Only you would defend vanilla!" Aunt Daphne shrugged in exasperated surrender. "You know, there's not much point in possessing wealth if one doesn't spend any of it. And if I know Raleigh Alden, he won't be spending a penny more on you than is absolutely necessary to keep body and soul together. I suppose gossiping is a cheap form of entertainment, but I prefer theater tickets, myself. And with Flint, I'm sure I'll be sitting in a box seat." By this time, Aunt Daphne had worked herself up into a frenzied state. Her voice rose in pitch and volume with each passing sentence. "Why, you and Raleigh deserve each other!"

"Aunt Daphne, please control yourself. I'm sorry I have vexed you so. I know you don't mean half of what you say."

"Don't I?"

"Well, I don't care what you say about Raleigh Alden. I have no interest in him whatsoever." Eleanor spoke the words as an honest attempt at truth, but her heart's increased thumping betrayed her tongue.

"Is that so?"

"It's true." Eleanor swallowed her mixed emotions. On the one hand, it felt good to hear Aunt Daphne pair them together. On the other, since he had betrayed her with his snobbish attitude, Eleanor didn't want anything more to do with him, even though she had to fight the feelings in her treacherous heart.

"I don't consider a snob like Raleigh as more than an acquaintance kind enough to lend me books from his personal library," Eleanor protested.

"A nice snob, eh? A contradiction of terms, indeed. I must say that after this conversation, I'll have to agree that it's high time that you returned to your home state. I'll send your father a telegram today telling him so. And I'll help you pack your bags."

Watching Aunt Daphne's newly developed eagerness for her to depart, Eleanor felt a sudden twinge of regret. "Perhaps I was a bit hasty. I do need to finish Vera's order."

"Never mind that. Neither I nor you will be sewing another stitch for any Alden—or for anyone who is a companion to them." With a firm motion, Aunt Daphne crossed her arms over her chest. "I won't even consider fashioning her maids' uniforms. Not even if she begs."

"But Aunt Daphne, she's your best client. Didn't you always say that a good businesswoman never lets her personal opinions and feelings interfere with a sale?"

"I said a lot of things. Things I'm beginning to regret. Besides, once I'm Mrs. Flint Jarvis, I'm not sure I'll have time to keep the shop open."

"But the shop is your life!"

Aunt Daphne set her lips firmly. "It is now, but that can change. Lots of things can change. Very quickly."

Eleanor tried not to show how upset she was at her aunt's

turnaround. Couldn't she see that Eleanor only cared about her welfare? She opened her mouth to argue, but her aunt's eyes had turned cold and hard. To debate would be futile.

❧

The next day, Raleigh knocked on the Kerrs' door and announced himself to their maid by handing her a calling card. After she excused herself, he remained on the stoop and tried not to let his expression reveal his great anticipation. He hadn't seen Eleanor in so long. Too long.

His mother's words resounded in his ears with the accuracy of a phonograph recording: *Everyone at the party could see that you have developed great feelings for Eleanor.* The recording continued. *I suggest that you make your intentions known to Eleanor.*

He had been an unbearable snob. He was only grateful that Eleanor hadn't been present to hear him make such foolish remarks about her station as a seamstress. Indeed, how could he have said such a thing and still call himself a Christian?

He had denied his true feelings and compounded his mistake by distancing himself from Eleanor in questioning her station. More admonitions from Mother played in his head. *I think you protest too much, Raleigh.*

If he had any doubts after speaking with his mother, the Lord made the message even more clear to Raleigh as he read his daily devotions: "There is neither Jew nor Greek, there is neither bond nor free, there is neither male nor female: for ye are all one in Christ Jesus." Galatians 3:28 had held no special interest or significance to him until he crossed that verse more times than he cared to recall over the past week. The Lord used it—along with his mother's wise counsel—to show him that his attitude toward Eleanor needed to change. Perhaps as did his view of many other people, as well. Raleigh sensed that the Lord would make those people apparent to him as he continued his spiritual walk.

Eleanor imagined that his profession lent itself to developing a prideful spirit, especially when a man enjoyed as many court victories as Raleigh. Ridding himself of that pride wouldn't be easy. But he resolved to shed it in obedience. Thankfully his first assignment would be easy. By reaching out to Eleanor, the blissful rewards promised to be boundless. He allowed himself a contented sigh.

He reached for his waistcoat pocket and extracted the seventeen-jewel Swiss watch that was an inheritance from Grandfather Alden. Where was that maid? Did she tarry because he had caught the Kerr ladies unaware?

Raleigh noticed the Kerrs' window box. They had made an effort to beautify the tiny patch of nature in front of the row house. The windowsill planter contained a cascade of white petunias backed up with black-faced blue pansies. English daisies flanked the box on both ends.

The front door creaked open. Raleigh looked at the direction of the sound and noticed that the maid was leaning out the doorway, wearing a cautious look on her face. "I'm sorry, Mr. Alden, but the ladies are not available at present."

Raleigh couldn't believe the maid. Surely Eleanor would be eager to see him, anticipating that he would be bearing news about Flint Jarvis. "Surely Miss Eleanor Kerr will see me."

She shook her head. "I'm afraid not, sir. Neither lady is available today."

"Perhaps I might call another time. When do you suggest might be suitable?"

The maid looked unsure. "Excuse me, sir." She disappeared again, leaving Raleigh to wait on the front stoop. He felt foolish standing alone in front of the house. Passersby looked at him as though he had taken leave of his senses.

"I'm sorry, sir," the maid said upon her return. "They were not able to provide me with a better time."

"I have no special need to see Miss Daphne Kerr, but if you

might suggest a time I can speak with Miss Eleanor Kerr, I would be grateful."

"I'm sorry, sir, but Miss Eleanor Kerr will be leaving for Louisiana within the week, and she will not be available to take any callers before she departs, sir."

Raleigh felt his jaw drop before he could contain himself. So Eleanor was to depart in a week's time? Without telling him? Without so much as a written good-bye? What was the meaning of this? He forced himself to regain his composure.

"Could you tell Miss Eleanor Kerr that I am here to see her on important business?" he asked. "She will understand my meaning."

The maid looked distressed but excused herself so she could comply. During her absence, Raleigh wondered what Eleanor was thinking. How could she plan to leave on such short notice and without even finding out about Flint?

The maid returned. "I'm sorry, sir, but the answer is no."

He decided to hit Daphne where she lived. "Tell Miss Daphne Kerr that I am here to settle my mother's bill."

"Yes, sir." The maid let out a tired sigh. Raleigh felt sorry for her, but he had to see someone in the Kerr household, one way or another.

Her prompt return left him with hope until she shook her head. "Miss Daphne Kerr said she has not yet tallied the latest charges, and she has asked to settle them with you when she sees you at your mother's next appointment. Good day, sir."

The faithful maid shut the door in his face before he could come back with any retort.

Some lawyer I am! I can't even find the right words to handle a delicate situation in my personal life, yet clients depend on me every day in a court of law.

Sensing defeat, he slumped his shoulders and headed toward his carriage. He felt chagrined that his driver had to witness his unsuccessful attempt to meet with two seamstresses.

Thankfully, Jeters was known for his discretion.

"Where might I take you now, sir?" Jeters asked.

"Home. I just want to go home." Raleigh heard the weariness in his own voice.

In the carriage, he thought about the events that had transpired. There was no love lost between Daphne and him, but Eleanor was another matter. Why had she refused to see him? She had humiliated him, yet instead of feeling justified anger, he felt guilty. Why?

Then he remembered his conversation with his mother. She had accused him of being an unbearable snob, an accusation he richly deserved. Had Eleanor discerned his hidden emotions toward her? How could she have? He had always been careful not to reveal anything to her but kindness and friendship. Trained in the ways of the courtroom, Raleigh prided himself on being able to hide his thoughts. Such restraint could make the difference between winning and losing a case. Why did he have the distinct feeling that Eleanor knew more about him than he realized?

Yet even if she knew his feelings of superiority, certainly that discovery would not be enough to convince her to leave town abruptly. Why? Why was she leaving?

If a heart could feel a literal ache, Raleigh's did at that moment. He knew in that instant that he didn't want to lose Eleanor. Not then. Not ever. He had to get her back. But how?

An idea occurred to him.

"Jeters?"

"Yes, Mr. Alden?" he asked over the *clip-clop* of the horse's hooves.

"I've changed my mind. I'm not ready to go home yet. Take me to the harbor."

eleven

Raleigh made his way to Flint's office, hoping against hope that Flint might be there.

Lord, I wouldn't be doing this except that Eleanor asked. I pray we're doing right in finding out more about Flint Jarvis.

His prayer was cut short as the carriage stopped. Moments later, Raleigh found an office front etched in gold letters with JARVIS SHIPPING, MR. FLINT JARVIS, PRESIDENT.

"At least he does, indeed, have an office," Raleigh mumbled under his breath. He turned the handle and entered.

A plain secretary who looked too thin was typing a letter. She turned from her work. "Good morning. What may I do for you today?"

"Raleigh Alden here." He handed her a business card. "I am looking for Mr. Flint Jarvis."

She took the card and read it. "I don't recall scheduling an appointment for you."

"That is because I don't have one. But I am known to Mr. Jarvis, and I'm sure he will see me if you will just let him know I'm here."

She set the card on her desk. "I'm sorry, but he isn't here."

"I can wait."

"Indeed, but you will be waiting until close of business today. We don't expect him in at all."

"Not at all?"

"No." Neither her face nor voice held any sign of apology.

"Tomorrow, then."

"I don't think so, but let me see." She consulted a book

135

bound in black leather. "No, I don't expect him in for at least a week or two."

"But he's in town."

"I am not at liberty to say." Her voice took on an edge. "What is your business here? Perhaps his assistant, Mr. Stone, can help you?"

Raleigh tried to hide his irritation under a pleasant expression. He almost told the secretary never to mind but decided that perhaps Flint's assistant could shed some light on the matter. "Very well. I'll see him."

"Indeed? How kind of you." Her voice reeked with irony.

Raleigh bit back a stinging retort. He supposed she was only doing her job as a gatekeeper. He eyed the office door to her side that was labeled MR. LEE STONE, then watched as she thumbed through the pages once more. "I'm sorry, but his schedule for the day is full. You'll have to wait. Next week, perhaps?"

He thought about Eleanor's imminent departure. "Certainly not. My business is urgent."

She shook her head. "Mr. Stone is very strict about—"

Raleigh had had enough. Without another word, he burst into Lee Stone's office. Though he expected to find Mr. Stone engaged in a meeting or even to discover a vacant office, instead he found a man with gray hair and a matching mustache running an adding machine. The man, presumably Lee Stone, rose to his feet. "See here! What is the meaning of this?" His voice rang with a British accent. "Who are you?"

Raleigh handed him a business card. "Raleigh Alden, Esquire, sir."

The secretary was on his heels. "I beg your pardon, Mr. Stone. This man has been quite obnoxious, and he broke into your office without my leave."

Lee read the card, "Is this about some kind of lawsuit?"

"No."

"Then just what is your business with me, that you felt the need to enter my private office?"

"My business is urgent, but I promise not to take much of your time. I am a businessman as you are, and I know that time is money."

Mr. Stone waved his hand to dismiss his secretary, who nodded and shut the door behind her. He remained standing and didn't gesture for Raleigh to take a seat.

Raleigh didn't waste any time. "Where is Mr. Jarvis?"

"I say, that is none of your affair."

"I understand from your secretary that he isn't expected to be in the office over the next few weeks, yet I know for a fact that he is in town."

"I don't conduct business every day that I'm in town."

Raleigh took in a steadying breath. "Could you tell me where he is, then?"

"You seem to know his whereabouts. Why don't you go and find him yourself?"

"You don't know where he is, do you?"

"Are you here concerning Jarvis Shipping or about a personal matter?"

"Both."

"Then I recommend that you find Mr. Jarvis and discuss your business with him. Clearly, I can be of limited, if any, assistance." Mr. Stone sat back down in his seat. "As you can see, I have a business to run and accounts to balance. Good day." He leaned over his machine and punched in a number.

"But—"

"Good day." Mr. Stone's voice was firmer than ever, and he didn't bother to look up from his work.

Raleigh knew the next step would be for Mr. Stone to call in his secretary and to instruct her to summon the police. The time had come to admit that his mission had failed. Without another word, he made his exit.

"I trust your business went well, sir?" Jeters asked moments later as Raleigh climbed into the carriage.

"No, I'm afraid it didn't. Take me to the residence of Flint Jarvis on Charles Street."

The ride up the hill from the harbor took twenty minutes. Jeters had quite a time navigating the crowded warehouse district. The streets were narrow and filled with many carts and wheelbarrows. Charles Street was a desirable address, but Raleigh was taken aback by the large row house—four windows across when most had only two or three—where the carriage stopped. "Are you sure this is it?" he asked Jeters.

"Yes, sir."

Raleigh emerged from the carriage and noted that the residence seemed grand for one engaged in ordinary employment. Flint Jarvis was becoming more and more puzzling with each stop Raleigh made.

A moment later, Raleigh tried not to appear impatient when he lifted the brass door knocker, which was in the shape of a lion's head.

Flint's butler soon answered. Unlike the Kerrs' maid, he was quick to inform Raleigh that his master was absent.

"Is there a good time for me to return?" Raleigh asked as he handed the butler a calling card.

"I have no firm time to suggest, sir. Mr. Jarvis left early this morning, and I have not seen him since."

"And he didn't say where he was going?"

"I am not at liberty to say, sir."

Raleigh wondered what he meant but knew that to press the matter with a servant paid to protect his employer's privacy would be pointless. "Thank you and good day."

Thoroughly vexed, Raleigh decided he could either comb the streets of Baltimore in hopes of running into his acquaintance, or he could try visiting Flint's aunt. He decided on the latter.

"The residence of Miss Jessica Jarvis, please," he instructed Jeters.

Since Raleigh's mother and Miss Jessica had been friends for decades, Jeters knew how to lead the carriage to the brownstone home on East Mount Vernon Place. This time, when Raleigh got out of the carriage and knocked on the door, the maid granted him entrance and led him to the formal parlor overcrowded with antique furniture and bric-a-brac. He didn't have to wait long to see Miss Jessica.

"Raleigh. What brings you here?" Miss Jessica looked as well as ever. Her once-black hair was streaked with white, reminding Raleigh of a skunk. He wondered why someone so unlike a skunk would be trapped into bearing hair with such odd coloring. "Would you care for tea?"

"No, thank you, Miss Jessica. I won't be staying long. In fact, I regret to tell you that this isn't entirely a social call."

She gasped. "Is everything all right? Your mother isn't ill, is she?"

"Oh, no, no. It's nothing like that. Mother is as feisty as ever, I'm happy to say."

She placed a thin hand on her lace-covered chest and sank into a red velvet chair. "I'm glad to hear it. She told me all about the dinner party. I wish I could have been there. A previous engagement I couldn't break precluded my attendance."

"Oh?" Raleigh hadn't been aware that Miss Jessica had been on the invitation list. "Well, everyone understands." He took a seat on the sofa by the picture window.

"At least I got to hear an excellent secondhand account of the party. Hearing your mother tell it was almost like being there myself."

"Yes, she does have a talent for reciting social events. I surmise that if she had been born a man, she would have made an excellent newspaper reporter."

"A man, indeed. If the suffragettes have their way, women

will soon have the right to vote, then who knows what liberties they will take with the country next."

"Perhaps a woman can be president one day."

Miss Jessica gasped. "Please! Don't even speculate on such a travesty!"

Raleigh suppressed a grin and changed the subject. "I'm sure Mother told you that your nephew Flint kept everyone enraptured with his accounts of travel."

"Everyone except the woman she invited him for—what is her name?" Miss Jessica rubbed her chin and looked at the ceiling. A light of remembrance touched her wrinkled face, and she lifted her forefinger. "Ah, yes. The new little seamstress. Eleanor. I've got to commit her name to memory. I thought I might engage her to sew my Christmas dress. I understand she's quite good."

"Yes. Vera was very pleased with the dress that Eleanor sewed for her for the party. I thought it looked quite nice on her."

Miss Jessica's eyebrows arched. "Did you now?"

Raleigh wasn't sure what she implied. "Uh, yes."

"Your mother will be pleased that you have taken notice of Vera. Finally."

"She will?"

Raleigh didn't think it was possible for her eyebrows to rise any higher, but they managed. "You didn't realize?"

Had his mother told everyone in the world about her attempts at matchmaking? "Realize what?"

"I spoke out of turn. Don't mind me. I'm just an old lady with her ramblings. Now as much as I enjoy a visit from a courtly man such as yourself, you said this is not a social call. What is your business with me?"

"I want to know about your nephew."

Miss Jessica shrugged. "What is there to know? It's not as though he's afraid to talk about himself."

"Of that fact, I am well aware. At least as far as his travels are concerned. But he is reticent of offering any details when it comes to his job."

"So? What of it?" She touched the side of her spectacles, adjusted them lower on her nose, and looked over the top of them at him. "Don't you know that it's considered rude to pry into the nature and source of a man's livelihood?"

He didn't let her statement or her gesture intimidate him. "Forgive me, but I hope you will hear me out and give me whatever insight you can. For you see, I am out to prove that your nephew's honor is unimpeachable."

Her posture softened. "I see. And just who is questioning his honor?"

"I'm not at liberty to say. But I assure you that your trust in me will not be misplaced if you can tell me what you know."

She readjusted her spectacles to their proper position. "Very well, then."

"Miss Jessica, I was wondering what you know about your nephew's work. What does he really do to support such a lavish style of life and with more than enough time to travel the world?"

She cleared her throat. "He has quite an ordinary job."

"Indeed? A job that allows him never to appear in his office and to gallivant all day about town as though he had not a care in the world?" He tried to keep the accusatory tone out of his voice.

"You are a successful lawyer, but you have time off from your work." She sent a prolonged glance to the clock on the fireplace mantel. "Take today, for example."

"Yes." He cleared his throat. "But naturally, I do hold to a schedule. If I didn't, I would soon find myself without clients."

She looked at him quickly before averting her eyes. "I do admit, I am proud of Flint's success. He has done quite well for himself."

Years of courtroom experience led Raleigh to recognize her

change in tactics as an avoidance measure. "Yes. Too well."

Her eyes narrowed. "I don't think I like what you are implying."

"Neither do I. That's why I'm hoping you can shed some light on the matter."

Miss Jessica's manner took on a cautious air. "What does his career matter to you?"

"People I am fond of might be hurt, that's why."

She chuckled, and her thin body relaxed. "I understand your fondness for Vera, but I assure you, my nephew is not a threat to you there."

Vera. Why did she keep talking about Vera?

"So if you'll excuse me," Miss Jessica rose from her seat, "I must prepare for tea. Flint is due here any minute for our weekly visit, and considering your rather impertinent questions, I suggest you depart before he arrives."

"I beg your forgiveness if my questions seem discourteous, Miss Jessica. Perhaps I am impolitic to put you in the position of responding to them." Raleigh fiddled with the brim of his hat. "But on the contrary, rather than wishing to depart, I am pleased to learn that I might have a chance to see Flint myself. I've been searching for him all day, and I came here as a last resort. It seems that the Lord has guided me to this place at this time after all."

"Don't bring the Lord into your tawdry investigation. If you have anything to say to my nephew, it won't be in my parlor. Good day, Mr. Alden." She turned her back to him and glided through the door.

"But—"

"Lacy!" Miss Jessica called.

The maid materialized almost instantaneously. "Yes, Miz Jarvis?"

"See Mr. Alden to the door."

"But if you will just let me see him for a moment, I'm sure

we can clear everything up. If your nephew is the gentleman you say he is, wouldn't you welcome the chance for him to clear any doubts about himself?"

"If you insist on speaking to him, you can wait on the front porch. I will not be party to any exchange." She exited the room before he could bid her a good afternoon.

Although Raleigh felt odd standing on the stoop, thankfully he didn't have to wait long. Flint rode up in his carriage and exited with all the verve of a diplomat on an important mission. At that moment, Raleigh wished he could turn around 180 degrees and forget he had even started the whole mess. But then a picture of Eleanor popped into his head, and he knew he had to press on for her sake.

Raleigh stood with straightened shoulders, waiting in anticipation.

Flint spotted him and waved. "Raleigh, old man!" he said as he ambled up the walkway. "What are you doing here on my aunt's porch? Isn't she home?" His heels *clacked* on the steps.

"She's home, all right. She sent me out here to wait for you."

"How unmannerly of her. I'm surprised. Usually she has the southern hospitality thing down pat. Well, I won't have anything to do with keeping a guest waiting outside in the afternoon heat. Come on in with me."

Flint's enthusiastic greeting almost made Raleigh feel guilty, but he knew he had to complete his errand. He followed Flint into the house.

"Lacy!" Flint called, even though no one was anywhere in sight, "I'm here!" He didn't wait for a response before motioning for Raleigh to join him in the parlor. "I was just out duckpin bowling. The last game of the season." He sat in a wingback chair. "A great sport. Seems to be catching on."

Raleigh nodded. John Van Sant, the manager of Diamond Alleys in Baltimore, had reduced the size of standard bowling pins that year at the suggestion of some customers. The idea was quickly evolving into an established sport. "I'll have to try it sometime."

"Yes, you must," Flint enthused as his aunt entered.

Both men rose from their seats.

"Aunt Jessica! Look what the cat dragged in. Left it on the porch, at that." He strolled over to his aunt and gave her a kiss on the cheek.

"Hello, Flint." Miss Jessica's tone was warm toward her nephew but then froze. "Raleigh." She nodded ever so slightly. "You're still here."

Flint looked from Raleigh to his aunt. "Is anything the matter?"

"Why don't you find out for yourself? If you'll excuse me." Miss Jessica exited.

Flint turned to face Raleigh. "See here, old man, what is this all about?"

"I'm afraid I am not here on a social call. I need to know, Flint, what exactly do you do to earn your income?"

"There's nothing like getting right to the point, is there, Counselor?" His expression wore a combination of amusement and curiosity.

"Time is of the essence. If I'm not able to give certain people assurances of your honor, both of us may lose everything that means anything to us."

"I'm afraid I don't understand what you mean. Furthermore, what right have you to question my honor?" The muscles in Flint's jaw tightened.

"Whether I have the right is not the question." Raleigh made sure to keep his tone level. "You can trust me when I say that once our conversation is complete, you'll be glad I asked about the source of your income."

"So that is what this is about? You're concerned about where I get my money?"

At that moment, the maid entered with a tray holding tea and sandwiches.

"I didn't ask for tea." Flint's voice had lost its charm.

"I know, sir. Miss Jessica said to bring it in."

"That's fine," Flint said. "I'll serve us."

She set down the tray on a low table made of cherry wood.

"That will be all." Flint motioned for Raleigh to return to his seat, and he did the same as the maid nodded and made a silent exit.

Flint's gaze followed her out of the room. "She's burning with curiosity."

"On behalf of your aunt, no doubt. At least she will have nothing to report. Nothing that your aunt doesn't already know."

"So she is aware of the nature of your visit?" Flint's sharp tone indicated his displeasure.

"I spoke to her out of desperation. I searched all over town for you and failed to find you until now. If you had developed the habit of checking in with your office each day instead of disappearing, I wouldn't have had to resort to intruding on your aunt."

"Rudeness is never excusable. But if you must know, I have done nothing illegal. The source of my income is perfectly legitimate," Flint assured him as he poured two servings of tea into hearty cups fashioned of solid white china. "You need not worry. My honor is intact."

"Then why doesn't it appear so?" Peeved, Raleigh took his tea without sugar or cream in spite of the fact that under more pleasant circumstances, he would have asked for both.

"And why, may I ask, doesn't it appear that I am honorable?"

Trying to calm himself and to appear sociable, Raleigh took a sip of the bitter brew, then set down his cup. "Appearances count, and though you may relish the role as a man of mystery, I'm afraid Baltimore society doesn't take kindly to real-life rogues."

Flint rose to his feet. "How dare you!"

Raleigh stood. "I beg your pardon." He decided that another tactic was in order. "Flint, am I right to assume that you are a Christian?"

"Of course."

"Then may I remind you of a verse that contains much wisdom, one that I find useful as I practice law. In 1 Thessalonians 5:22, we read: 'Abstain from all appearance of evil.'"

"Are you calling me evil?"

A female voice interrupted. "No, I don't think he is."

Flint turned to face his aunt, who had just entered. "Aunt Jessica, I beg your forgiveness. This discussion is entirely improper anywhere, especially in your very parlor." He turned to Raleigh. "I ask you to leave this instant."

"You can force Raleigh to leave, but that won't solve a thing." Miss Jessica brought herself up to her full height. "Flint, you have deceived everyone long enough. It's time for you to tell the truth."

twelve

As Raleigh watched the confrontation in Miss Jessica's parlor, he realized that he suddenly seemed small before the domineering woman. Flint exhaled an audible breath. "Aunt Jessica! Surely you jest."

She looked down her nose through her spectacles at him in the same manner she had exercised earlier with Raleigh. "No, I am not speaking in jest. You need to tell him everything."

Flint bristled. "But there is nothing to confess. I am a perfectly honest man who has done nothing wrong."

"Agreed," Miss Jessica said.

So Flint's aunt knew whatever secret he was keeping! Raleigh didn't like the feeling of being deceived.

"I think the fact that I am a respectable gentleman is all anyone needs to know." Flint's jaw muscles tightened.

"I believed that argument at first," Miss Jessica told him, "and I'm sorry to say now that I went along with it. But no more." Her look reminded Raleigh of a schoolmarm chastising a wayward boy for putting a frog in her desk drawer. "Clearly, Raleigh's visit here shows that the situation has changed."

Flint shook his head at his aunt. "I don't think so."

"Are you contradicting me?"

"No, ma'am."

"Good. For your mother, may the Lord rest her dearly departed soul, would find such impudence abominable."

Flint, usually so self-assured, stared at his finely crafted shoes. Seeing him so chastened seemed almost comical.

"Now then." Miss Jessica's voice remained firm. "You have a

choice. Either you can tell him or I will. Which will it be?"

As he watched their exchange, Raleigh's curiosity was piqued to a height he never could have imagined. At least he wouldn't have to wait long to have his questions answered.

Flint darted his glance toward Raleigh, then to his aunt, then back. Finally he let out a defeated sigh. "All right, then. You will feel like a fool when you find out what my big secret is." Flint's eyes had taken on a steely glint. "As Shakespeare once wrote, you are making much ado about nothing."

"I'll take that chance."

"We may as well sit down," Flint suggested.

The men waited for Miss Jessica to take a seat first. "That's quite all right. I'll leave you alone. I shall be in the garden if you need me."

The men bid her farewell, then sat down. Raleigh contemplated taking the remainder of his tea but decided the idea of lukewarm liquid wasn't appealing at the moment. He sat back in his straight-backed chair as much as was possible in hopes of putting Flint at ease.

"Care for more tea?" Flint asked.

"No, thank you."

"Suit yourself." Flint poured the beverage into his waiting cup. Raleigh noticed that hardly any steam resulted and decided he was glad he had passed on the refill. Raleigh guessed that Flint welcomed the diversion. The task kept him from having to look Raleigh in the eye.

"I recently came into an inheritance from an uncle I never knew." Flint looked at the teapot as though he were breaking the news to it rather than Raleigh.

"An inheritance? Well, aren't you the lucky fellow? But how did you come about gaining an inheritance from an unknown relative?"

Flint shrugged. "He was a bachelor, and my mother was his only sibling. She mentioned him from time to time, but he never set foot on American soil as far as I know. He was a trader in the West Indies."

"A profitable enterprise, then."

"Very much so." Flint's gaze caught Raleigh's before he stirred milk into his refreshment. "I received a significant fortune and part of that shipping concern."

Raleigh quickly put two and two together. "Which is why you have an office at Pier 7."

"Yes." Flint took a sip of brew. "And contrary to your beliefs, I do appear there when needed."

Raleigh remembered that Eustis had never seen Flint anywhere near his office. "Not often?"

"Not often."

"I must say that is odd."

"To a real businessman, yes."

Raleigh crossed his arms, hoping the stern gesture would prompt Flint to speak out of discomfort or embarrassment. Silence didn't linger long before proving to be his friend.

"Raleigh," Flint asked as he leaned his back against the chair, a gesture Raleigh knew was contrived to feign confidence. "I must ask what development caused you to decide that you had to know about my affairs at this point in time."

Raleigh mimicked Flint by settling in his own seat. "For the woman you love. I don't want to see her hurt."

"The woman I love?"

"I know you've been courting Daphne Kerr."

"Eleanor told you."

"When you're courting as heavily as she says you have been, how do you expect to keep it a secret?" Raleigh couldn't help but expand on the thought. "Why would you even want to keep it a secret?"

"I don't. I am quite fond of Miss Kerr. In fact—" He clamped his mouth shut.

Raleigh leaned toward Flint. He placed one elbow on his

knee. "Never fear. I am not Miss Kerr's guardian, and I am not here to ask your intentions. However, she is the aunt of someone I am very fond of, and I would hate to see either Kerr woman hurt by anyone." He balled his hand into a fist and propped his chin upon it.

A little smile touched Flint's lips. "Well, old boy, you say you are not her guardian, but you certainly are acting as though you were. Both women are lucky to have a friend like you."

"Then you understand my point of view."

"Yes. And I have to admire you. Not everyone would be willing to confront a man just to protect a woman who's not his wife, mother, or sister. That said, I want you to keep what I am about to tell you in the strictest confidence because I assure you, should my courtship with Daphne Kerr progress, she will be apprised of any information she needs to know."

"Understood." Raleigh sat back and nodded. "Keeping confidences is one key to success in the legal profession." He kept his lips in a straight line, so Flint wouldn't see how anxious he felt. Raleigh wondered if Flint was about to reveal that he was a smuggler, a bootlegger, or worse.

Flint returned his nod but didn't speak right away. "The fact is, I know nothing about the business, and, shamefully, I seem to have no aptitude for it."

"A man of your means and wit? Surely you exaggerate."

"I'm afraid you are wrong to place such confidence in me. Oh, I tried to run the business. I assure you, I tried. But I made a mess of things. Thankfully, one of my uncle's faithful employees, Lee Stone, possessed the knowledge to make sure I didn't ruin the enterprise." He looked down at the floor in a gesture of obvious embarrassment. "Ever since he came to my rescue, I have depended on him and a circle of other trusted employees to keep my business afloat."

Raleigh hesitated. He knew the dangers of putting one's

livelihood into the hands of others, even those who seem trustworthy. He had a feeling that Lee Stone would be sure to mention his visit to Flint's office and decided he'd best come clean. "I met Mr. Stone today when I went to your office in search of you." Before Flint could ask more, Raleigh hastened to add, "He seems efficient enough. He was running an adding machine during my visit."

Flint chuckled. "That sounds like Lee."

"While he seems quite competent, are you sure you're perfectly at home with the idea of giving him so much power over your business?"

Flint shrugged. "What other choice do I have?"

"For one, you could sell out."

Flint thought for a moment. "I have too much pride to sell out now that I've found I have a sizeable source of income—something to pass on to my heirs." Flint's gaze met Raleigh's. "You see, I've never had that before." He paused. "I know you're smart, Raleigh. Your reputation is that of one of the most wily—and honest—lawyers in town. You can go to your practice each day with the confidence that you won't come out looking foolish."

Raleigh felt a twinge of sympathy. "Since you have shown courage in expressing yourself to me, I would be wrong not to admit that I've lost a case or two in my time."

"Of course. No one—not even you—always wins."

"No, but I've never lost a case because I whiled away all my time at local taverns."

Flint winced. Raleigh almost regretted making his observation aloud, but perhaps hearing the truth could hurt enough for Flint to change his ways.

"Maybe not," Flint said, "but you were born to wealth. Of course, you're going to succeed. You know something, Raleigh? Before I came into my unexpected inheritance, I had no way of traveling at all. I was barely scraping by at a dull job making less than eight hundred dollars a year. I had no dreams of travel, and my hours were long. Now I can do as I please with no one to answer to." His eyes darted toward the door through which his aunt had exited. "Well, almost no one."

Raleigh grinned. "Be thankful that someone cares about you. Loneliness is a terrible thing. Why do you think I pay Miss Howard to stay with Mother?"

"I suppose." Flint didn't smile as Raleigh expected. Instead, he seemed pensive. "As to not revealing everything about myself, I don't expect you to understand my point of view. And I'm sure some people doubt me, maybe even gossip about me. But I'd rather be thought a well-traveled man of intrigue than to be known of as a fool—even though I can take comfort in the fact that I am a rich fool."

Raleigh took a moment to digest the information Flint had just shared. "I must say, I'm relieved to learn the facts. If I were you, I wouldn't hide behind my embarrassment any longer. So what if others run your business? I have many clients who are in the same situation."

"Do you protect them?"

Raleigh considered his question. "Not really. Most people would find my business of civil law quite dull. Just lots of papers to shuffle from one place to another, all covered with Latin phrases that few outside the profession understand. So far I haven't been offered the chance to defend a guilty person. If I were, I'm not sure I would. I prefer to be on the side of right."

"But isn't it right to keep wrongdoers from suffering punishments that are too harsh to fit their crimes?"

"Yes."

"So isn't that part of your job? To keep everyone from discovering reality?" Flint gave him a sly smile as if to show he was in jest, but Raleigh knew that Flint believed his observation held a ring of truth.

"On the contrary, the essence of the legal profession is to find and to reveal the truth, not to diminish it." Raleigh rose from his chair. "Which is why I want you to do something for me."

When Flint stood, he adopted the posture and speed of one far beyond his years. Surely the conversation had drained him of energy. "Haven't I made enough concessions for one day?"

"I'm glad to see your capacity for wit is returning. What I want you to do will be of great benefit to you and to the one you love."

"Do you think my chances with her would be increased if she knew the facts? Do you really believe that?"

"I do." Raleigh's voice rang with the strength of the truth he knew.

"And my confession won't hurt your chances with Miss Eleanor Kerr, will it?"

"Since you have been candid with me, I owe you the courtesy of being just as frank with you. Yes, Eleanor will be greatly comforted to know the truth about you, and since I will be accompanying you to the Kerr house today, my chances with her will improve considerably." His heart did a funny flip-flop when he mentioned Eleanor's name in such close connection to his own. Somehow, it sounded perfect. Amazing, even. A wave of relief mixed with pleasure washed over him. Raleigh and Eleanor. Eleanor Alden. The combination sounded right.

"Today?" Flint's voice sounded like a jolt. "Can't this wait until tomorrow?"

"No. The sooner the better." He almost confided the fact of Eleanor's imminent departure but decided that such a ploy would make him look too desperate. Though he had gained respect for Flint during their conversation, they hadn't established trust to the level that Raleigh wanted to let Flint know just how much power he held over him at that moment.

"I don't know—"

"As much as this will benefit me, I wouldn't ask you to go if I didn't honestly believe it would help you, as well."

Flint didn't seem too happy. "If you insist."

Raleigh struggled to keep exhilaration out of his voice. "I'm afraid I must."

Flint took a moment to bid his aunt good-bye, then accompanied Raleigh into his carriage. The two men were silent during the brief trip, a development uncharacteristic for the garrulous Flint. Raleigh was grateful for the time to pray in silence.

Father in heaven, I pray that the Kerrs will see us. I try not to ask Thee for much, but please, grant me the favor of Eleanor. I pray that though this is my will, that her ability to return my love is Thy will, as well. In the name of Thy Son, amen.

If Flint was aware of Raleigh's turmoil or if he experienced any of his own, his bland expression left no indication. Almost before Raleigh knew it, they had arrived at the Kerrs'.

ð

The maid entered the room where both women were working. Aunt Daphne had just begun sewing a lace blouse, and Eleanor was putting the finishing touches on an order she had promised to complete before leaving for Louisiana.

"Mr. Jarvis is here to see you, Miss Daphne."

Daphne gasped and rose from her sewing machine so fast that Eleanor thought she would knock over the chair. "Flint! Why, what is he doing here now? We don't have plans."

"He said he was here on business, ma'am."

"Business? Hmmm. Well, tell him I'll see him immediately."

"Oh, but Miss Daphne, he brought Mr. Alden with him."

It was Eleanor's turn to drop the dress on which she was working. Made of slick satin, it slid down her legs and landed on the floor. Eleanor made a quick motion to retrieve it.

"Tell Mr. Alden to go away," Aunt Daphne said with a sharp tone.

"I tried, but it isn't working this time. Mr. Jarvis said that he won't come in without Mr. Alden."

"This time?" Eleanor asked. "He was here before?"

Aunt Daphne nodded. "Yes. I told him we wouldn't see him."

Eleanor wondered what to do. She desperately wanted to speak with Raleigh. If she didn't see him now, perhaps the opportunity would never again present itself. And she had a feeling that their business had something to do with Flint's secret. She decided to intervene. "Please, let's see them, Aunt Daphne."

"Are you daft? I thought he had hurt you."

"But he wouldn't be here with Mr. Jarvis if it wasn't important. I think we should hear what they have to say."

"Well, perhaps I can agree to see them alone."

"No," Eleanor said too hastily. "I mean, I should at least give him the consideration of one last good-bye."

"If you insist." Despite her aunt's curt words, Eleanor could see relief soften the woman's features. She never wanted to forego an opportunity to see Flint Jarvis.

"Very well," Aunt Daphne instructed. "Escort them into the parlor. We'll be in shortly."

"Do I offer tea, ma'am?"

Aunt Daphne glanced at the clock. "No, it is too near dinner. If they delay, we can invite them for a meal. Cook is preparing roast beef tonight, so there should be enough to set two extra plates."

"Yes, Miss Daphne."

Eleanor folded the satin garment, rose from her seat, and placed it in her chair before consulting the mirror to confirm the state of her appearance. She was glad she had chosen to wear her best housedress that day. She wished she could excuse herself long enough to change into her Sunday dress but realized that to do so would make her appear too contrived—and too interested in Raleigh's visit.

She darted her gaze at Aunt Daphne and saw that she was preening with as much enthusiasm.

"Are you ready?" Eleanor asked. "You look wonderful, by the way."

Aunt Daphne swept her gaze over Eleanor. "As do you."

Eleanor smiled. She was enjoying the truce she and her aunt had reached in unspoken agreement, so much so that she knew she would miss her once she left.

"In fact, you look so lovely today that he might try to convince you to stay," Aunt Daphne suggested.

"Oh, pshaw."

But indeed, that is what she truly desired. Psalm 37:4 popped into her head: "Delight thyself also in the LORD; and he shall give thee the desires of thine heart."

"Flint!" Aunt Daphne said as soon as she crossed the threshold of the parlor. "How nice to see you. I wasn't expecting you."

Not caring about Flint, Eleanor cut her glance to Raleigh. His eyes lit as their gazes met, though his expression seemed to be touched by remorse. Then she remembered how she had eavesdropped on his conversation. She wondered if regret showed on her face, as well. Though she may have appeared to be calm on the exterior, her increased pulse upon seeing him again revealed to Eleanor her secret feelings. Why had she become so vehement with her aunt and insisted on returning to Louisiana? She didn't want to go back. She wanted to stay here in Baltimore. Her new home. Where Raleigh was.

Aunt Daphne touched her hair. "I'm sorry I don't quite look my best."

"But my dear," Flint quipped, "you always look your best."

Aunt Daphne giggled like a shy little girl being asked what she wanted for Christmas. She sat down, and the others followed suit.

"So tell me what your business is." Aunt Daphne sent Raleigh a cold look.

Flint garnered her attention. "I'm aware that my style of life doesn't appear to be consistent with my income."

"Oh, that." Aunt Daphne sent Flint a dismissive wave of her hand. "Really, people are just too nosy." She sent a frigid stare to Eleanor, who squirmed.

"I'll make myself brief. My uncle left me an inheritance."

"Is this a recent development?"

"Two years ago. Before then, I—I was a clerk." Flint looked at his shoes. For the first time in memory, Eleanor felt sorry for him.

"But you're a big man in shipping now," Aunt Daphne urged.

"Yes. Yes and no. Well, I have an interest in a shipping concern, but I have nothing to do with its operations except to sign the occasional paper and review quarterly reports. And I should have admitted that from the start. I beg your forgiveness."

"What should I care about how you run your business or how you came to enter it? Such concerns belong to men, not to me."

"I would expect other women to think that, but not you." He rubbed his thumbs together but looked Aunt Daphne in the eyes. "Daphne, you are such a talented businesswoman. You know the ins and outs of your shop and can recite facts and figures from memory. Quite impressive, really."

"Quite necessary, actually."

He chuckled. "I feel like such a dimwit in comparison to you."

"A ridiculous notion."

"Not when one considers that I depend on others to operate the business that keeps feeding my wealth—wealth I never earned. Rather than a man of considerable talent and wit, you must think me a fool."

"A fool? No, I think you are one of the luckiest men I know."

"But how can you respect a man with such little talent as I possess?"

"You underestimate yourself," she protested. "As long as your business is legitimate—and obviously it is—I don't care how involved you are in the day-to-day operations, whether you or someone else runs it, or what you know or don't know. Can't you see, Flint? I don't want to be with you because of your business, but because of the man you are. And nothing will ever change that."

Relief flooded his face. "Indeed?"

"Indeed." Aunt Daphne rose.

He leaped to his feet and strode toward her. "But others might think—"

"Who cares what others might think? I don't care what kind of fool you say you are. I love you with all my heart."

"And I love you."

Frozen in her chair, Eleanor watched the couple stare into each other's eyes. She couldn't help but feel a twinge of envy despite her happiness for Aunt Daphne. Oh, to enjoy such unblemished love! If only she could rid herself of her feelings toward Raleigh!

She sighed. At least someone was experiencing a happy ending. But not her. And it could never be her. Eleanor rose from her seat to make a silent and hasty exit. No matter how much she loved her aunt, she couldn't stand being witness to so much happiness when in only a few days her own world would change irrevocably. She would never see the one she loved, ever again.

thirteen

"Wait!" Mr. Jarvis's voice cut through the air in the parlor.

Eleanor stopped so abruptly that she knocked her shin into the tea table. Cups and saucers rattled together. After assuring that no china had been damaged by her near mishap, she looked up at him.

Flint lifted his forefinger. "There's more."

With the spell between the couple broken, Aunt Daphne startled as though she was regaining her senses. "There certainly is. What brought all this on, Eleanor? Why do I have the distinct feeling that you had something to do with this?" She stared at Raleigh. "And what about you?"

"Now, now, dear." Flint patted her on the hand. "That's what I wanted to talk about. Raleigh and Eleanor were, indeed, instrumental in bringing on this confession, but I don't want you to harbor any ill will toward either one of them."

"But why shouldn't I? I could have lost you."

"I'm not so sure about that, unless my own false pride had been in play. They were right, you know. I had been carrying a burden—the burden of deceit—that I knew had to be lifted eventually. I just kept putting off that eventuality. Now that everything is out in the open, I see how ridiculous I was to be worried." He turned to Raleigh. "I want to thank you for forcing my hand, old boy. You did me a favor."

Raleigh nodded once. "I'm glad, but the one you need to thank is Eleanor."

"So I was right." Aunt Daphne's tone was less forgiving. "You are the one who stirred the brew."

"Don't be so hard on your niece, my dear," Mr. Jarvis admonished. "You should be grateful that she cares about you so much."

Aunt Daphne glanced downward and her posture softened. "I suppose. . ."

"No supposing about it, my dear," Mr. Jarvis said. "It's true."

"But Eleanor shouldn't have poked her nose into my business and dragged Raleigh into the thick of it."

"Whatever you think, won't you forgive them both? For my sake?" Mr. Jarvis implored.

Aunt Daphne's lips tightened as she thought about his plea. After a moment, she nodded. "All right. For you, I will."

"Thank you, Aunt Daphne."

"Thank you, Daphne," Raleigh added. "My mother and I hold you in regard, and we, too, want to remain on the best of terms."

Eleanor remembered what her aunt had said earlier about not wanting to sew another garment for an Alden or even for Vera. She wondered what her response would be.

"All right, then. I forgive you both for prodding into our affairs. I suppose it is better to get everything out in the open. Knowing that Flint was concerned about the way I felt, I regard him more highly now than ever."

She gazed up into his eyes, the love unmistakable. He returned her look.

"I do believe I would care for a glass of lemonade." Eleanor tilted her head toward Raleigh as she stepped to the door. "Would you like to join me?"

Raleigh cut his gaze to the loving couple and nodded. "A glass of lemonade sounds delightful." He followed Eleanor.

She hadn't counted on being alone with Raleigh but found she didn't dread the opportunity. Instinctively, she headed to the back of the house toward the kitchen, then took a turn.

How could she expect someone of Raleigh's esteemed position to accompany her to the kitchen?

As Aunt Daphne had mentioned, Cook was preparing roast. Since the cut of beef was substantial, delicious cooking aromas had been swirling through the house for some hours. Inhaling, Eleanor realized she was hungry. She wondered if Aunt Daphne would ask the men to dinner. She was tempted to broach the idea but knew it really wasn't her place.

She happened to see the maid in the midst of refreshing the flowers on the dining-room table. "Would you bring Mr. Alden and me some lemonade in the drawing room?"

"Yes, Miss Eleanor."

Soon they were in the drawing room, sitting across from each other in front of the unlit fireplace. Raleigh was the first to speak. "That went better than expected."

"I must say, it certainly did go well."

"You weren't surprised."

"I can't say I was taken aback, although I hadn't realized their feelings had developed to such an extent. I'm happy for Aunt Daphne, truly. And now that you have found out about Mr. Jarvis, I'm happy for him, too."

"Good." He exhaled. "Finding out about him was quite a trial."

"And I thank you. I feel so much better now. I can be happy knowing that Aunt Daphne isn't marrying someone who is suspect."

"Even though I proved you wrong by showing that Flint isn't a smuggler or worse, I admire you for wanting the best for your aunt. You are a fine woman, Eleanor Kerr."

"Thank you." Though hardly as romantic as the words she had heard Flint Jarvis exchange with her aunt, pride swelled in Eleanor all the same. Raleigh's sentiment possessed more substance. She wished she could return his compliment, but his other, unflattering words—overheard as they had been—

had hurt too much. "I'm not of as great a substance as the women of Baltimore society, I'm afraid."

His dark eyebrows shot up. "On the contrary, I think you surpass them."

"Don't exaggerate for the sake of flattery, please." At that moment, the lemonade arrived, but the beverage couldn't have been colder than her tone.

"I assure you, I do not exaggerate."

She softened her demeanor. "Then thank you."

Raleigh took a full glass from the tray. "Oh, there are some pretty ladies here, some smart ones, some devout ones, some silly ones, and some who possess a few of all these traits." He shrugged.

"But none who have caught your fancy."

"None." His voice dropped to a whisper.

Eleanor took a sip of her own lemonade and found it too tart for her taste. She ran her tongue over her teeth in a vain effort to wash away the sourness as she set her glass on a crocheted doily on the table. "You left someone in Florida, then."

"No, indeed. One or two of the ladies there caught my eye, but I didn't feel the emotion—or the Lord's leading—required for me to court either with any seriousness." He took several swallows of his lemonade, apparently not minding the tartness.

Eleanor waited. Perhaps if she didn't look too eager, he would speak up and try to convince her not to leave.

"I miss some things about Florida, but now that I'm back in Baltimore, I find I feel right at home." As he continued on a monologue of the virtues of Florida versus the virtues of Maryland, she tried to keep an interested look on her face. If he had any emotion to share with her, he wasn't going to reveal it. Had she misread him so badly?

After he had nursed two glasses of beverage, Eleanor knew she couldn't detain him longer. "I have enjoyed this afternoon with you, Raleigh, but I'm afraid this is good-bye. I am return-ing home next week as planned."

Following her lead, he rose from his seat. "I'm sorry to hear that we couldn't entice you to stay in Baltimore."

She hesitated. Did he really want her to stay as a romantic interest, or was he just being polite? Could she hope? "No. No, I can't." Eleanor left before he could say more. She didn't want him to see her cry.

&

That evening as he read his devotions, Raleigh couldn't con-centrate. The conversation with Eleanor lingered too heavily on his mind. Some of the statements she had made struck him as strange, indeed. Why had she asked him about other women? And what was that business that she wasn't as good as they were?

He kept reading, even going so far as to deviate from his current study of 1 Kings to flip through both the Old and New Testaments to see if he could find some words of advice. What would the Lord tell him? Nothing he landed on seemed to apply.

"I must be obtuse today." Self-disgust permeated his voice. "Who cares?" he muttered. "No one else is around to over-hear me."

His mind began clicking everything into place until he remembered the conversation he had engaged in with his mother. A conversation he wished he could erase forever, but he could not. A conversation during which he was repri-manded by his mother, and rightfully so. But hadn't he made amends by doing Eleanor's bidding? He couldn't imagine any other circumstance where he would have investigated Flint. But Eleanor had asked, and for her, he did the deed.

Yet Eleanor wasn't convinced that she was good enough for him. He drummed his fingers on the arm of his chair. Someone must have told Eleanor about what he had said. He didn't bother to contain a gasp.

That had to be it! Yes!

But whom? Surely his mother would have been more discreet. She may have been upset with Raleigh, but her pride would have kept her from revealing outside of the family anything about Raleigh that shamed her.

Then who? Vera. He rubbed his shaven chin, which had grown stubble over the course of the day, with his thumb and forefinger. Could she have overheard them? But after the dinner party, Raleigh thought Vera understood that he simply felt no romantic attraction for her. Vera was a lovely woman, not mean-spirited enough to say something to hurt Eleanor, for whom she had obviously developed a fondness. He imagined Vera would miss Eleanor more than Daphne.

Monroe. Perhaps he had told Eleanor. He never seemed to hold her in particular regard. Just as quickly, Raleigh dismissed the possibility. Even if Monroe had overheard him talking—a situation not uncommon for a servant—he had not the sharp disposition to cause trouble. Yet even if Monroe had been so unkind, Raleigh doubted Eleanor would have paid him much heed. Still, if he had said something. . .

He would confront Monroe the next day. In the meantime, he needed to go to the Lord in a spirit of humility. Flint may have thought himself a fool, but Raleigh saw that he, not Flint, was the real fool.

Lord, I give Thee my false pride. Show me Thy way.

෨

Only a few miles away in a small room in a row house in the city, Eleanor was praying just as fervently. Why hadn't Raleigh professed his love to her? She could see his feelings written on his face. And she loved him. No matter how much she fought it, she did. Seeing her aunt and Flint Jarvis that day, so enraptured with one another with a love so pure, only made her feelings toward Raleigh more difficult to deny.

Yet despite the odd feeling she had as they shared lemonade together, he apparently hadn't been moved enough to make a declaration.

She knew why. No matter what his mother said, Raleigh didn't think she was good enough.

But he had said she was a fine woman. And his voice had been filled with conviction, too. He wasn't lying when he said it or wasting words on false flattery. He had really meant it.

So where did this leave her?

Father in heaven, was I too hasty in making the decision to leave here? I feel no sense of peace about my decision. What is wrong? Please, Lord, show me Thy way.

૨

The next morning, Raleigh met with Monroe in his office before his first appointment of the day. "Monroe, did you by chance overhear a conversation between my mother and myself last Tuesday when Miss Vera was out on an errand?"

Monroe gazed at the ceiling as he thought, then looked at Raleigh with a gaze of deference. "No, sir. Was I supposed to?"

Raleigh tried again. "You can tell me the truth. I know you are privy to conversations around the house. If you overheard, I understand. But I need to know the truth."

"Yes, sir. But no, sir, I didn't hear anything. When Miss Vera was out, I was tending to your wardrobe. I remember."

Raleigh thought for a moment. Monroe, indeed, had tended to his wardrobe that day, and he would have been too far away to overhear them talking. So he must be telling the truth. And that meant that if he didn't overhear the conversation, then he couldn't have said anything to Eleanor. "Very well, then." He was about to dismiss Monroe when he had another thought. "Was anyone else in the house that day? I know it was the maid's day off, and Cook was engaged in the kitchen."

This time Monroe didn't hesitate. "Yes, sir. Miss Eleanor

came by. I found her in the foyer. I asked if I should announce her, but she declined. She said she had left something at home and went back out to get it."

Aha. "So you didn't hear her knock?"

"No, sir."

"Did she seem upset?"

"Yes, sir. She seemed distracted. I assumed she was embarrassed about forgetting some of her work."

Raleigh's stomach knotted. If Eleanor had thought he was a snob, his conversation, never meant for her ears, confirmed her suspicions about his feelings—feelings that were part of his past, not of the love he held for her now. Shame filled his being as he thought about how he must have hurt her.

Father in heaven, canst Thou forgive me? Can Eleanor forgive me?

He kept his expression placid so as not to reveal his turmoil. "Very well, Monroe. You are excused."

So Eleanor must have let herself in, then overheard them. No wonder she was upset, and no wonder she had been acting strangely. He had to think of something. He couldn't let her go back home with anger on her mind. In fact, he couldn't let her go at all.

૨૭

Eleanor arrived at church with slumped shoulders. This was to be her last Sunday in Baltimore. She would miss the Christian community she had grown to love. But she couldn't stay. Yet she still felt no sense of peace about leaving.

Aunt Daphne tugged Eleanor's gloved hand, which clutched her Bible. "There's Flint, just as he promised." She motioned for Eleanor to follow.

"Is that Raleigh sitting beside him?"

Aunt Daphne shrugged and kept walking.

Eleanor tried to put on a happy face. If Raleigh didn't return her feelings or if he simply refused to acknowledge them, then she wanted no part of sitting by him in church. Yet when she slid into the pew, she developed the distinct feeling that she had been set up as Mr. Jarvis and Aunt Daphne maneuvered for Eleanor and Raleigh to sit by one another.

"What are you doing here? I know you have your own church. Did Mr. Jarvis put you up to this?" she hissed at Raleigh.

"He did ask me to attend today's service with him, then dine at his home afterward. I thought the least I could do to repay for my intrusions earlier in the week was to accept his invitation."

Eleanor couldn't avoid breathing in the familiar scent of bay rum he wore. She would miss that fragrance. And she would miss Raleigh. But she could never let him know. Aggravated, she opened her Bible to a random passage. Remarkably it landed on the tiny book of Jonah. She tried in vain to concentrate on the words.

Jonah. He was running away. Just like Raleigh and I are.

The thought only served to upset her more. She shut the book with more snap than holy parchment pages deserved. She took out her Sunday white lace fan and waved it over her face.

"Today's message is on the subject of denial," the Reverend Spencer began after the singing of hymns—which Raleigh joined in with vigor—and the passing of the collection plate. "Have you ever denied your love for someone?" the minister asked. "For someone important? For someone who could—and would—change your life, if only you would let Him?"

Eleanor squirmed. Surely, the Reverend meant the Lord Jesus. Of course, He had the power to change anything. With God, all things are possible.

To Eleanor's surprise, the Reverend Spencer recounted the gospel account of Peter's denial of Jesus. Peter denied Jesus thrice, yet Peter became an important figure in the early church. The minister then went on to compare the love that Christians are to show one another to the love that Jesus showed Peter in the face of betrayal. After a forty-minute sermon that managed to fly with amazing speed, he ended by asking, "Are you denying someone your love today?"

Even though the love in question was *agape* rather than romantic, Eleanor couldn't help but feel that the Lord was speaking to both her and Raleigh through the sermon. She stole a glimpse at Raleigh from her peripheral vision. He kept his expression blank, but his eyes almost looked as though they were about to mist. Knowing that no modern man would want to be caught dead fighting such emotion, she stared back at the pulpit. Had the Lord gotten through to him after all?

After the benediction, Raleigh leaned toward her. "May I come by your house this afternoon?"

She nodded. Sunday dinner promised to be the longest on record.

ತಿ

If he had had any doubt before, Raleigh knew what he had to do now. He had to convince Eleanor to stay. There was no obstacle to their love except his own unwillingness to put asunder his pride. And what Eleanor had overheard. He flinched each time he remembered his words.

Lord, I pray that Eleanor will forgive me!

She was waiting for him when he arrived at the house. Nervousness clutched at his stomach with intense ferocity.

"Thank you for agreeing to see me today," Raleigh said.

She nodded. Her response was the appropriate one for such a noncommittal greeting, but noncommittal wasn't what he desired. "Eleanor." He didn't waste time discussing the weather or any insignificant matter. If he did, maybe he would lose his nerve—and his chances with her. He moved closer and took her hands in his. Was her heart beating as fast as he thought his was?

"Yes?"

Her encouragement gave him the fortitude to speak. "I've been a fool. I know you overheard the conversation I had with my mother. I'm so sorry for everything I said. Mother was right. I was an unbearable snob. I have been praying to the Lord, and He has shown me how utterly indefensible my attitude was. I beg your forgiveness for how I hurt you."

"So—so you know? You know that I eavesdropped?" Embarrassment made itself apparent in her expression. She stepped into the parlor and Raleigh followed.

"I didn't put two and two together until last night."

Her face flushed. "I'm sorry I eavesdropped. How rude you must think me. I am the one who should be apologizing to you and, indeed, I am. Can you forgive me?"

"Of course. If someone had been talking about me in such a manner, I would have taken pause to listen in as well." He squeezed her hands. "I'm only sorry that I caused you such hurt. You have no idea how many times I have wished I could take back that day!"

"I can see that I was too hasty in judging you."

"I was not too hasty in judging you."

"What?" She tried to pull her hands out of his, but he held tightly.

"Whether you are a seamstress, a maid, or to the manor born, I knew from the day I first met you that you are a splendid woman—a woman any man would be lucky to have as his wife."

Her eyes widened, but she remained silent.

"I should have listened to my heart from the start."

"What are you saying?"

"I'm saying I don't want you to go," he blurted.

"But—but my train ticket—"

"If they won't give you your money back, I'll refund you double."

"So you're resorting to bribery?" Her tone was teasing.

He smiled. "I love you, Eleanor Kerr. And I always will."

"Oh, Raleigh, I feel the same about you. And I have for a long time. How could we have almost fallen victim to love's denial?"

"Our injudicious pride, that's how. But the Lord showed us a better way."

"We'll have to thank the Reverend Spencer."

"Indeed, I think I'll make out a bank draft to the church as soon as possible. Or at least give him a generous sum of money for performing our marriage ceremony come spring— if you will agree to become Mrs. Raleigh Alden."

She gasped. "Are you sure?"

"What kind of answer is that?" He snapped his fingers. "All right. You want me to do this the right way." He smiled and got down on one knee. "Miss Eleanor Kerr, will you do me the distinct honor of accepting my plea for marriage?"

She didn't pause. "Yes!"

"I will cable your father immediately to ask his blessing."

"I know we shall have it."

Raleigh rose and rushed to embrace her. As he brought his lips toward hers, she didn't hesitate to respond. How long he—indeed, Eleanor, as well—had waited to seal their bond. A bond that pride had almost broken but that God had clearly ordained. Her sweet spirit, her soft lips, her warm embrace, her heart for God—he would relish each day with Mrs. Raleigh Alden. Forever.

A Letter To Our Readers

Dear Reader:

In order that we might better contribute to your reading enjoyment, we would appreciate your taking a few minutes to respond to the following questions. We welcome your comments and read each form and letter we receive. When completed, please return to the following:

Fiction Editor
Heartsong Presents
PO Box 719
Uhrichsville, Ohio 44683

1. Did you enjoy reading *Love's Denial* by Tamela Hancock Murray?
   ❑ Very much! I would like to see more books by this author!
   ❑ Moderately. I would have enjoyed it more if

   _____

   _____

   _____

2. Are you a member of **Heartsong Presents**? ❑ Yes ❑ No
   If no, where did you purchase this book? _____

   _____

3. How would you rate, on a scale from 1 (poor) to 5 (superior), the cover design? _____

4. On a scale from 1 (poor) to 10 (superior), please rate the following elements.

   ____ Heroine   ____ Plot
   ____ Hero   ____ Inspirational theme
   ____ Setting   ____ Secondary characters

5. These characters were special because? _____

_____

_____

6. How has this book inspired your life? _____

_____

_____

7. What settings would you like to see covered in future
   Heartsong Presents books? _____

_____

_____

8. What are some inspirational themes you would like to see
   treated in future books? _____

_____

_____

9. Would you be interested in reading other **Heartsong
   Presents** titles? ❑ Yes ❑ No

10. Please check your age range:

   ❑ Under 18   ❑ 18-24
   ❑ 25-34   ❑ 35-45
   ❑ 46-55   ❑ Over 55

Name _____

Occupation _____

Address _____

Virginia

4 stories in 1

*S*panning the innocent age of tall ships through the victory of WWI, this captivating family saga celebrates the rich heritage of Virginia through four romance stories by author Cathy Marie Hake.

Innocence and intrigue, heartbreak and hope mingle in a world where God's grace and the power of love transform lives.

Historical, paperback, 464 pages, 5 ³/₁₆" x 8"

_____

Hearts♥ng

Any 12 Heartsong Presents titles for only $27.00*

HISTORICAL ROMANCE IS CHEAPER BY THE DOZEN!

Buy any assortment of twelve *Heartsong Presents* titles and save 25% off of the already discounted price of $2.97 each!

*plus $2.00 shipping and handling per order and sales tax where applicable.

HEARTSONG PRESENTS TITLES AVAILABLE NOW:

(If ordering from this page, please remember to include it with the order form.)

Presents

Great Inspirational Romance at a Great Price!

Heartsong Presents books are inspirational romances in contemporary and historical settings, designed to give you an enjoyable, spirit-lifting reading experience. You can choose wonderfully written titles from some of today's best authors like Peggy Darty, Sally Laity, DiAnn Mills, Colleen L. Reece, Debra White Smith, and many others.

When ordering quantities less than twelve, above titles are $2.97 each.
Not all titles may be available at time of order.

HEARTSONG
PRESENTS

If you love Christian romance...

You'll love Heartsong Presents' inspiring and faith-filled romances by today's very best Christian authors...DiAnn Mills, Wanda E. Brunstetter, and Yvonne Lehman, to mention a few!

$10.⁹⁹

When you join Heartsong Presents, you'll enjoy 4 brand-new mass market, 176-page books—two contemporary and two historical—that will build you up in your faith when you discover God's role in every relationship you read about!

Imagine...four new romances every four weeks—with men and women like you who long to meet the one God has chosen as the love of their lives...all for the low price of $10.99 postpaid.

To join, simply visit www.heartsong presents.com or complete the coupon below and mail it to the address provided.

Mass Market 176 Pages

✂ -

YES! Sign me up for Heartso♥ng!

**NEW MEMBERSHIPS WILL BE SHIPPED IMMEDIATELY!
Send no money now.** We'll bill you only $10.99 post-paid with your first shipment of four books. Or for faster action, call 1-740-922-7280.

NAME _____

ADDRESS _____

CITY _____ STATE _____ ZIP _____

**MAIL TO: HEARTSONG PRESENTS, P.O. Box 721, Uhrichsville, Ohio 44683
or sign up at WWW.HEARTSONGPRESENTS.COM**

ADPG05